The Shakespeare Reader
and other Christmas Tales

Maren C Tirabassi

To Mary —
Have a Merry Christmas!
Maren C Tirabassi

DEDICATION

For John and Deirdre Nettleton, whose acting has brought Shakespeare to life. We celebrate your diamond anniversary this Yuletide.

CONTENTS

Introduction

Some say that ever 'gainst that season comes
Wherein our Savior's birth is celebrated,
This bird of dawning singeth all night long;
And then, they say, no spirit dare stir abroad,
The nights are wholesome, then no planets strike.
No fairy takes, nor witch hath power to charm,
So hallowed and so gracious is the time.
Hamlet, *Act 1, Scene 1*

I love Christmas stories – short stories and long stories, ghost stories and children's stories, tall tales and winter tales, the history of carols, the mythology of Grinch, Nicholas and Scrooge, the screenplays of memorable movies, and those television specials everyone else has forgotten.

I love Christmas stories. I *like* the works of William Shakespeare, but I am surrounded by people who *love* the Bard. That's how these stories began – as Christmas presents. While I have no intention of sending out into the world holiday ramblings that star our family pets, my relatives, or the vagaries of parish life, I hope that these tales entertain your December evenings.

"The Dark Ride" is about the wife of a retired high school English teacher who tries to make a go of a Shakespeare-themed amusement park in rural New Hampshire and what happens one solstice afternoon. "Enter Friar, Stage Left" is a contemporary re-telling of *Romeo and Juliet* from the clergy perspective. "The Shakespeare Reader" introduces a gentleman who fancies himself a sleuth because he recognizes the Shakespeare plots underlying the comings and goings of his Harvard Square neighbors.

Many people helped me put together this little book. For wrangling the publishing process, I'm grateful to Maria Mankin and Don Tirabassi. For amused encouragement, Matthew Tirabassi. For creating such a beautiful cover, Joe LaRue. For being the best beta readers out there, Victor Floyd, Lou Grosso and Nancy Hardy.

And I am grateful to you, dear reader, for passing this way.

THE DARK RIDE

Double, double toil and trouble;
Fire burn, and cauldron bubble.
Macbeth

"I wash my hands of it," his wife said and by that she meant all of it. All the trouble. All the double toil. All the taped witches chanting. By "all" she really meant "All" in a rather specific way – "All the World's a Stage," the theme park into which they had poured their time, their money, their parents' money, their children's money, most of their hopes and almost all of their marriage.

Maybe something was left.

He was an expert on amusement parks. He wrote his PhD on their history before the teaching certificate enticed with its security, and long before all those high school football players took Shakespeare for an easy grade because they had seen "MacHomer," the Simpson send-up of the Scottish King. They thought he was talking about Bart rather than Bard! But he liked kids and he was willing to reach them. Kids liked amusement parks. Amusement parks are a world away, and what young person doesn't need a world away? He had.

When shall we three meet again – in thunder, lightning, or in rain? Again witches, this time in parting. He had parted, escaped really, from the fearsome family of his childhood to amusement parks and Shakespeare plays. Why shouldn't he marry the two?

Not exactly an expert on marriage.

If Gwynne were true to herself, she'd needed escape too, not from furniture breaking against the walls but from financially generous neglect that purchased lessons, memberships in clubs, clothing the envy of all her friends ... or rather money for the clothing that was the envy of all her friends. Not once did she remember, "I'll come with you to the mall." Not that. Not company. She found her world between the covers of a book. Not much different than a tilt-a-whirl. She didn't have the testosterone for whack-a-mole. Think of that – low on testosterone and married to a man named Macbeth.

Earliest heritage for amusement parks was the Bartholomew Fair, England, 1133. The oldest identifiable park was Bakken, north of Copenhagen, Denmark, opened in 1583. A theme park is more elaborate yet, a specific type of amusement park, so much more intricately wedded to, well, a theme. Like Shakespeare.

Her husband was going to single-handedly kill the theme park and who knew the old man had so much blood in him!

Amusement parks also claim to be the descendants of the pleasure garden movement. Especially popular at the beginning of the Industrial Revolution, they were places of escape from grim urban environments. Tivoli Gardens (again Copenhagen – the Danish are a wonderful people ... think of Legos, well, think of *Hamlet*) dated from 1843. He wanted to take her to Copenhagen for their honeymoon. She wanted a beach in the sun by turquoise waters. Maybe snorkeling. Read a trashy novel. Their finances stretched to Niagara Falls.

Amusement parks flourished in the United States. By 1919 there were almost two thousand of them. Americans were a demanding people. They didn't want to wait for a carnival or Chautauqua to come to town, the annual summer fair date to dawn. They wanted carousel on tap. Amusement parks parked. They were found often at the end of railway lines, or trolley lines or streetcar lines...

This amusement park was probably the end of the line for these two people.

There were dark decades – fires plagued the wooden rollercoasters and the Depression of the 1930s and World War II in the 1940s depressed attendance. Fifties families were not on Ferris wheels eating cotton candy and laughing under the stars – they were sitting around the moonshine of the television. Then came 1955 and Disneyland. Disneyland completely changed the landscape of the amusement park industry. Now miles of undeveloped land surrounded theme parks. They were hidden. Magical. Educational, even.

The summer before she and Mac met, he took a thumb and backpack tour of derelict parks in the United States to mark a silent salute of respect to their graves. Best were the abandoned but not built-over sites where the bones of an ancient roller coaster might rise in skeletal glory, or he could unearth a sign that said in peeling paint, "hot dogs, peanuts, and cotton candy." The trip took three months, and he did it instead of making money for his final year at college. He recounted this quest to a freshman he de-barricaded from her book while she took a break in the coffee shop that was one of his two part-time jobs. They sat over endless cups of dark romantic roast talking and listening to music that must have been popular at the time.

These were beautiful and tragic places, he told her. She knew his eyes were beautiful, dark and liquid ... not at all forecasting that someday he'd be so nuts he could see Banquo stalking their breakfast nook. Someday, he told her, they would go to Tanzania. Gazing at her, he continued, "In Tanzania we can see an incredible derelict amusement park."

They had never gone. She should have recognized that it was the not-making-money part of that summer that was precedent setting. Like his namesake, he could use some girding, some "manning up." *Yet do I fear thy nature; It is too full of the milk of human kindness to catch the nearest way* or any dollar. But then, again, they would not need to take a trip to see a derelict amusement park. They were creating their very own.

But she was wrong about not traveling. Thirty years later they did take another trip. It was just after the retirement deal that exchanged one less teacher with seniority for George Macbeth's opportunity to be to be full-time crazy. They traded the house where they'd raised their kids for a motor home and went on the road investigating "their" dream of creating a new world, a new life. They actually went to Holy Land USA, the Holy Land Experience, and Dinosaur World. They went to SeaWorld and Busch Gardens, both well noted for their educational aspects. She should really count her blessings that Shakespeare did not lend itself to thousands of animals, fish or, in fact, sea life of any kind.

Fairies. Horses. That was about it.

Heads of asses.

Theme parks. Tie one to a video game, to a popular book. Potter Park. Twilight Tivoli – she could imagine a vampire plunge, a full moon fun house. Secretly she thought there just might be a market for a Shades and Glades of Gray for a certain adult audience. But Shakespeare?

One of the significant changes that came with the ascension of Disney was seclusion. The thrills of theme park rides are obscured by landscaping, re-enforcing the feeling of entering a magic kingdom. Not the end of the trolley, but the destination of an airplane trip. The more expensive, the more desirable. Follow the money, Petruchio. Obsessive compulsive cleanliness, smart advertising, and annual new rides keep people coming back. Follow the money, Shylock. After the wonder of Disneyland, Disneyworld and its offspring, many other parks tried to copy its ideas, such as the hub-and-spoke layout and sub-themed lands or sections. They popped up across the country.

And he was determined to create one.

Why didn't he get a franchise? Why didn't he open another Dollywood? No. Another Bible park – maybe the Travels of Paul? No. The Inquisition? After all, in Salem, Massachusetts, witches made buckets of money every October while commemorating intolerance and cruelty to old women and wise women and men, all in the name of Halloween. No. Why not a Bear-baiting park? That was nearly Shakespearean. No. No, she didn't mean it – but maybe she did.

MacBeth thought that smartphone-implanted young couples would be excited wandering around the Forest of Arden, pinning and hunting love notes on the trees. OK. She admitted the publicity was good when this amusement was posted and tweeted as LGBTQI friendly.

"All the World's a Stage" was in the middle of nowhere, too, which in her mind was the definition of New Hampshire. He got that part right.

Canst thou not minister to a mind diseased,
Pluck from the memory a rooted sorrow,
Raze out the written troubles of the brain
And with some sweet oblivious antidote
Cleanse the stuffed bosom of that perilous stuff
Which weighs upon the heart?

Gwynne or George – Macbeth or his Lady – of which was it written?

In the theatre, actors and stagehands always call it "the Scottish play." Maybe Gwynne should have called herself the Scottish wife, and never taken his ill-omened surname at all.

It was the afternoon of the solstice and cloudy all day at that. It would be as dark as dark could be. The grounds were closed tight for the season. Their little house, not much larger than the mobile home but with an infinitely improved shower, was the only source of light. She guessed he was taking the Dark Ride, the one themed to ... the Scottish play.

Rides! He could lecture on their history as well – at length. The earliest ride was the carousel, and the carousel at All the World's a Stage was a spinning wonder of *Midsummer Night's Dream* characters. This Merry-Go-Round was aimed at the smallest of children. Little girls could ride on fairies and boys on Nick Bottoms or Pucks who "girdled the world" on an inner track that went twice as fast and required a safety harness. Twinkling lights portrayed Cowslip, Pease Blossom and their kind. Oberon and Titania were painted on the center post, in pursuit of each other but never touching.

Ferris wheels were rooted originally in the Fair tradition. MacBeth had pondered the theming of the Ferris wheel for a long time. He ended up naming each swinging seat with a different play and it became the ride that sent kids to research Shakespeare ... at least far as Wikipedia. Children who returned had told Gwynne they looked up *King Lear* and *Two Gentlemen of Verona* and *Titus Andronicus* and *Troilus and Cressida* and the Richards and Henrys to decide which one they wanted to ride. It was her suggestion that they create their own little catalogue of synopses in cartoon format and she found the art student who would do it cheaply just to be in print and on sale. A portfolio item is a portfolio item.

Grandparents bought these by the dozens – it was the fastest sell except for chocolate daggers, but once the information was that accessible they had to switch plays to protect youngsters from the gloomiest. *Titus* was replaced by *Romeo and Juliet* and was a big giggler for the middle school crowd, and *Merry Wives*, which sounded upbeat and maybe Christmasy, replaced *Richard III*. That attracted, according to Gwynne, no one but scholars, actors and Josephine Tey fans.

It was fun putting the Ferris wheel together. See, she was trying to be honest. She was really trying to be honest. She wasn't just jumping in a boat and floating down stream away from him like Ophelia.

A historic ride with an interesting past that he would describe at length to new New Hampshire friends was the roller coaster. A state with the motto "Live Free or Die" is accepting of small oddnesses in people who run businesses that employ their high school and college-aged children. Beginning as a winter sport in 17th century Russia, which has quite enough winter to support it, roller coasters were gravity driven railroads. With steep drops, sharp curves, and inversions, they were the first thrill rides. All the World had two. "O-yell-o" was a straightforward roller coaster they had purchased from a park that closed. They painted alternating seats white and black. Gwynne was firm; it was as close to the play's content they could go without being boycotted by a civil rights group.

The other roller coaster was his most recent pride and joy. It was a water ride, a significant financial investment. It was called "The Tempest," and it spun through both an enclosed section with suns and moons and stars, and splashed in pools. It was as twisted as the plot (if anyone who rode it ever knew the plot), but it was the final splashdown that always upset Gwynne. They came down in a pool full of books. *I've drowned my books*, says Prospero, and he means his scheming, his magic, his long dark search for revenge. But, yes, he literally says, *I've drowned my books*. Surely her Macbeth would know that it was the ultimate insult to a bibliophile. Surely, after all these years together and four children ... Miranda and Duffy and Ben (short for Benedict) and Harry ... he would know how much that image upset her! Surely ...

Other rides she liked much better. "Much Ado about Whirling" was their tilt-a-whirl. Gwynne liked spinning better than plunging, and there wasn't anything Shakespearean in it except the name. "The Tower of London" drop was a plunge ride but she had made him remove any reference to the deaths of little boys. Was he clueless? The whack a mole had villainous names like "Claudius" "Timon" "Edmund" "Regan" "Iago." There were variable point values, but the kids just learned the points rather than looking up the stories.

Then there was the Dark Ride. Dark rides are enclosed attractions where the park visitors ride in guided cars along a predetermined path through an array of illuminated scenes that may include abrupt lighting effects, animation, music, recorded dialogue, and creepy touching things. Tunnel of Love or Haunted House. This ride was the couple's namesake ride.

> *Tomorrow, and tomorrow, and tomorrow,*
> *Creeps in this petty pace from day to day*
> *To the last syllable of recorded time,*
> *And all our yesterdays have lighted fools*
> *The way to dusty death.*

Someone was knocking on the door. Gwynne looked up startled, realizing that her tea had long since gone cold while she waited for Mac to check the park and presumably take the Dark Ride on the solstice for the last of his discontented season. He should be back by now. She sat still and the knocking came again. She wasn't dreaming. She pulled her thick Scots sweater around her and ran fingers instead of a comb through her brush of graying auburn hair.

The young man was slim, wearing a yellow T-shirt with a Google logo on it. His green leather jacket was open to reveal this flash of sunshine and coxcomb. He had forgettable jeans, boots, one earring. Gwynne thought he looked a little like a parody of a modern young man. In her experience that meant he was an actor. His hair was a little on the long side, tucked behind his ears and he had a small pointed beard. A little affected, but his smile was warm. He seemed familiar but she could not place how she knew him. She scanned the yard behind him and stiffened. She didn't see a car and this was a long way from much of anywhere.

"May I help you?"

"Hi, are you the Globe and Rose people?"

"The Globe and Rose people? I'm sorry ..." she trailed off, confused.

"That's not the right name, is it? The Shakespeare Theme Park? Is it Lord Chamberlain's Men?"

"Lord ...? Oh. No, it's called All the World's a Stage. Yes, we manage the park. It's closed down for the winter months. Once there's snow and ice we can't run the rides. Are you looking for someone? For work? We don't get many off-season visitors out here."

"I've heard about it – your Shakespeare theme park. It's all about the stories, not like Stratford-upon-Tokyo or the Garden of Shakespeare's Flowers in Golden Gate Park. You have the most interesting re-creation since crazy Charles Lamb – well, not so crazy as his sister but still ..." he drifted off.

She waited. Scholar? The idiosyncrasies of both the autodidact and academy-taught were no stranger to her and she shared an arm's length but respectful fondness for Charles Lamb's struggles in life and his *Tales from Shakespeare*, out of fashion now, but genius in their own right.

He went on, "What a wonderful thing, a great diversion, a wondrous bauble – to make these strange old words the fun of real groundlings once again."

"Ah, ha." Her words were a place-saver. She didn't know what to make of him, no more than twenty-five certainly, out in the solstice darkening with no vehicle in sight. There were home invasions in the news. But this young man seemed harmless, with his big smile. Just a college kid. Mac would be home. No harm asking the boy in. Perhaps he was the kind of enthusiast Mac had been when he was in college, traveling around to see all those has-been amusement parks ... before he, like the Lambs, went a little nuts.

"My name is Gwynne Macbeth. Really." She saw his smile. "Please don't laugh – I know it is hard to resist, given ..." and she swept her hand around. The back of "O-yell-o" loomed in the fading sunset like an unnatural mountain, and the pink light of the dusk painted the alternating white girders into a strange bridge to fairyland rather than a secondhand coaster. "My husband is the theme park keeper, and he's out checking the rides before tonight's snow. He is an expert on all things Shakespeare and all things theme park. They are his twin enthusiasms. What brings you here?"

"I would love to meet him. May I wait?"

She hesitated for a minute. First she had to ask. "Your car?"

9

"Oh, I have my bike ..."

At her puzzled expression he continued, "My motorcycle. It's over there."

She could see it then, leaning against the tree, clearly silhouetted, and she wondered how she had missed it the first time. "Of course. It will be fine there. Will you come in for a cup of tea?"

"A cup of tea in Falstaff's Inn? I'm guessing you don't have sack?" He smiled so winsomely she opened the door and he came in, and with him so much chilly wind she closed the door quickly behind him. And there he was now. In. The hall was dark. She hoped he read her hospitality and did not sense her sudden nerves.

"Forgive me. The house isn't quite so period on the inside." Nor was she so much of a Merry Wife. It was a faux-Tudor-beamed facade, but most of the rooms were as twenty-first century cheap as they could be – IKEA furniture, iPad and laptop, books and papers strewn about, even the NatureBright Sun Touch lamp she'd purchased this week to try and keep them both from growing too sad from the financial failing or SAD with the seasonal falling. Ordinary rooms of an ordinary couple who had been married forty years. Photographs of their children, who loved them but who lived far enough away that they never visited All the World's a Stage. They were happier to put grandkids on a plane.

The kitchen at the end of the hall had wooden beams and a fireplace. It was just a regular fireplace. Not a walk-in. Next to it was the old dark range with a teakettle. A cooling apple pie gave the scent of home. Smelling and seeing through a visitor's eyes, she relaxed. It appeared a pleasant place, a happy place, even.

The young man sat down at the table, quite at home. Romeo surged up, mid-howl in the key of G and ready to sniff the newcomer. Romeo was an old plump blind beagle, and he had slept through both knocking and conversation, but, once awake, it was clear that age had not diminished his bay. A veritable beagle of the Baskervilles. Romeo approved the newcomer. The sound of the hunt shut off like an automobile alarm and Gwynne relaxed in spite of the December darkness smothering this shortest day.

"Sorry about Romeo. Do you mind? He's just a sweet old boy."

"Romeo, wherefore…are you?" the young man hunkered down and scratched the perfect place behind the ears. "A bit more of the Old Adam in you these days." He looked gently at the milky eyes. "Looks like he's been loved?"

"… and fed, I know. He used to run his table-scrap carbs off, but recently they're settling around his middle. I don't know what's keeping Mac. Would you like Scottish tea or green tea or I have some ginger tea as well."

"A cup of Scottish tea would be delightful. Thank you so much." He sat down and looked around. "How long have you been running the park?"

"We've been here ten years. Mac took early retirement from a teaching job. We spent a year trying to decide just what to do and have been here since then. After the losses of the recession and changes in entertainment patterns, we may not last another season." Why was she telling him this? "It's hard to make a go of a small park like this. We staff it with college kids but they go back to school so early. And, well, Shakespeare isn't a household word here in New Hampshire. Milk? Sugar?"

"Both. Thanks. Sorry it's not going well. Ten years is a good run for any play."

"Well, it's not really a play. It's a theme park. Of course, in the first couple years we had plays in the Little Globe, our performance and multi-purpose space – two each year, one by regional professionals, and one by high school kids. Mac directed the kids. Those, in a way, were grand days. It seemed to make sense that it was a Shakespeare theme park, if someone who came could see a play a couple times during the summer. Also, every day at ten and two in the Little Globe there were famous ten minutes scenes." She paused. "I acted in some of them. Old woman scenes. Juliet's nurse.

Iago's wife. Gertrude once – that was amazing. But we don't do it anymore."

"What do you do in the Little Globe now?"

"We show movies in the afternoon of very old productions of Shakespeare which are in public domain. On Thursday nights through the summer we arrange licenses for more famous or recent movie versions and show them to tourists who are visiting the lakes. Fun for the evening, especially for those whose annual vacation happens to a land on a rainy week."

Her face lit up a little. "And Mac's been slowly creating a prop and costume shop in the lower level of the Little Globe. Kids come in and play with tankards and daggers and wooden swords. They put ruffles around their necks, swing cloaks that are not as heavy as the originals, but give them that sense of ... well, swash. I guess that some of them imagine themselves vampires, since that seems to be the fashion of these times, but it doesn't matter. They are playing with their imagination not their little hand-held devices. I'm sorry," she blushed just a little, "you are getting quite a dose of my prejudice!"

"I'm interested, go on. I share a few of those prejudices myself!"

"Well, Mac planned to spend the winter painting wooden boards to depict scenery and so we could take kids' photographs. Some of the boards would be backdrops and we would pose kids in costumes, while some would have a hole for the face and the costume painted on so a quick pose would get a fun shot. He was especially looking forward to doing the balcony scene from Romeo and Juliet that way – with two head holes. Kids ... and adults, too ... would love playing around with that ...

O Romeo, Romeo, wherefore art thou Romeo?
Deny thy father and refuse thy name;
Or if thou wilt not, be but sworn my love
And I'll no longer be a Capulet.

"Mac wanted a piece of paper taped to the back side for those who wanted to say the lines themselves, or, for those who preferred to lip sync, a button to push for recorded voices.

... What's in a name? That which we call a rose
By any other word would smell as sweet;
So Romeo would, were he not Romeo called,
Retain that dear perfection which he owes
Without that title. Romeo, doff thy name,
and for thy name, which is no part of thee,
Take all myself.

"And finally, of course!
But, soft! what light through yonder window breaks?
It is the east, and Juliet is the sun.

"He was quite excited about it."

"But something happened?"

"Would you like some more tea?" she asked. He held out his cup. "I don't know what's taking him. Well, I do. He loves to take the Dark Ride. It's called 'The Weird Sisters' and themed to Macbeth. He made it himself – learned the technology from here and there, put more and more of it together in the evenings. He is always tinkering with it. Besides the Little Globe, it's his greatest achievement. The other rides may be named for Shakespeare plays but that's often just a bit of catchiness – a quirk. The Dark Ride is an adventure into Macbeth."

"What is it like, this Dark Ride?"

"Well, a dark ride is the term for any enclosed ride, you know, like a haunted mansion or well, Pirates of the Caribbean – the ride from which they made the movie?"

He nodded, although she wondered. Somehow she couldn't picture this young man in a Jack Sparrow audience.

"*Fair is foul, and foul is fair.* The witches' philosophy of life is printed in gothic lettering at the beginning of the ride. The cars seat as many as four, two in front and two in back, and run along an electrified track. As the car heads into the tunnel, the echo-audio says, '*Something wicked this way comes.*' Around the bend and there they are – the three weird sisters, stirring their brew. The text is all mixed up a bit and out of order – it's a theme park, you know, not an acting conservatory, and ..."

"Yes?"

"Well, Mac believed that if Shakespeare himself took bits and pieces of earlier stories, legends, even history, and made them his own, we can patch Shakespeare around, keep the heart, bleeding or otherwise, and have it true, in a certain sense, to the original."

The young man nodded thoughtfully.

"So, anyway, the witches' speeches are a bit cobbled together. The car on its track comes around the corner and the dark riders see three shadowy figures bending over a steaming cauldron. It's a stereotype but the witches are Macbeth's nightmare of lurking ambitions and fear of them. They are dark and hooded creatures whose faces never appear. The hoods really help; there is no need to synchronize lip movements to the recording. They have a touch of Dickens' Ghost of Christmas Yet to Come." Gwynne shook herself. Her words seemed to be bringing some unearthly premonition into her warm kitchen.

"And like that ghost, it is their hands that are revealed, stirring and pointing. One says, '*Grymalkin – Something wicked this way comes ... All hail, Macbeth, thane of Glamis!*' And another one intones '*All hail, Macbeth! Hail to thee, thane of Cawdor!*' And the third witch, after a pause says, much louder than the first two – '*All hail, Macbeth, that shalt be king hereafter! Banquo and Macbeth, all hail.*' So you see we've missed a lot that was already at the beginning ..."

"Yes, and maybe some that was unnecessary to the play anyway."

She looked at him oddly, re-considering his scholarly motivations, but he seemed absolutely sincere, so she continued. "Then a recorded voice is triggered in the seatback of each car that replies:

Stay, you imperfect speakers, tell me more. By Sinel's death I know I am thane of Glamis. But how of Cawdor? The thane of Cawdor lives, a prosperous gentleman, and to be king stands not within the prospect of belief, No more than to be Cawdor. Say from whence you owe this strange intelligence, or why upon this blasted heath you stop our way with such prophetic greeting. Speak, I charge you.

"Now, the majority of our visitors have no clue what any of this means, but the hollow sound of the words and ominous environment tell the story well enough."

"Groundlings. Of course. They always know without knowing," he offered.

"Then there's a plunge into the dark. The incline is maybe only three feet – not roller coaster dimensions at all – but the effect of it on a smoothly gliding ride is heart dropping. After that, the path twists and turns with eerie sounds and moving dioramas for a while. There's a spot-lit pantomime scene between Macbeth and Lady Macbeth, and again there is some of her actual speech with an echo effect added:

Come, you spirits that tend on mortal thoughts, unsex me here,
And fill me from the crown to the toe top-full of direst cruelty!

"Next comes a long bit with a bloody dagger hologram leading the way, the handle toward the front of the car. I think eventually Mac wants to fill that stretch of track with another scene but as we have it now, it suddenly turns completely black and there are sounds of a murder. Mac feels that a scene of Macbeth's hesitation wouldn't work for our jaded modern audiences who see grisly CSI scenes every night on television. He also wants the murder in the dark so that the riders are as confused as in a modern mystery – who actually murders Duncan – is it Macbeth or his cruel lady?

"When the car emerges into dim light, a crown is hanging over it. That scares people more than any murder scene. And they hear again as if from the middle of the very seat they are riding in. A male voice:

Methought I heard a voice cry "Sleep no more!
Macbeth does murder sleep," the innocent sleep,
Sleep that knits up the ravelled sleeve of care,
The death of each day's life, sore labor's bath,
Balm of hurt minds, great nature's second course ...

Then a female voice:

Will all great Neptune's ocean wash this blood
Clean from my hand? No, this my hand will rather
The multitudinous seas incarnadine,
Making the green one red ...

Of course, that speech is moved – it is not the Lady's, not yet."

Gwynne shook herself. Funny. It sounded like she was praising her husband's crazy vision of the rise and terrible fall of his namesake.

"Let's see. The death of Banquo is done in pantomime." There is eerie music while the ghost of Banquo and the visions appear in a curve. Do you understand?"

"Oh, yes," he said, "I see it in my mind's eye. Must be back to the witches."

"You know the story well. Yes, the witches and the prophecies. All of Macbeth's responses come straight out of the car making the riders feel as though they are Macbeth themselves, triumphant yet heading to certain doom, because of course, it is a tragedy."

"It is a tragedy."

"There is not a lot of focus on Macduff and the home invasion of his family." She paused nervously, and then hurried on hoping that he hadn't noticed. "Have I mentioned that stories about killing children are not really popular with parents? It's a ride in a theme park. And honestly, once we had named one of our children Duffy ... But still, I will say this for Macbeth. We sell many copies of *Macbeth* in the gift shop, and we can't keep the comics in stock. That question about who murders Duncan sends them to the easiest version the very minute they emerge from the ride."

"In the gift shop?"

"Well, as they say, duh."

The young man looked as if perhaps he didn't, as a rule, say "duh." "Do you have the suicide of Lady Macbeth in the ride? You didn't mention it and suicide's a sensitive issue these days."

She paused. "No, we don't. It's not for certain in the play. It is still argued by scholars." She sighed and continued more slowly. "We had two fundraisers the first two years. For those ... " she paused and then rushed on, "For those I acted out the scene on a platform in the tunnel. I didn't speak, and it was unclear in swirling scarlet robes what I was doing but the 'voice of Macbeth' intoned the lines:

> She should have died hereafter;
> There would have been a time for such a word. ...
> Out, out, brief candle!
> Life's but a walking shadow,
> A poor player that struts and frets his hour upon the stage
> And then is heard no more: it is a tale
> Told by an idiot, full of sound and fury,
> Signifying nothing ...

"It was very effective ... too effective the second time."

"How so?"

"There was a suicide in town the following week. It was the wife of a powerful man. They had both been at the fundraiser. It was never mentioned that there was some connection, but certainly Mac became stranger after that time."

"Did he blame himself or the ride?"

"Certainly he could not do that, could he? It's not like he suggested suicide for the wives of the wealthy and influential." They were both quiet for a few moments, and she watched the time slip past on the large clock. This was a patient young man. "'The Weird Sisters' is the most intricate ride, and Mac does keep adding bits to it and has plans for more. Like tonight, he often rides it by himself and I will admit ..."

Why was she admitting any such thing to this young man?

"I will admit that bothers me. I would prefer to have him engaged in another of the stories – a comedy or maybe a magical romance, *The Winters's Tale* perchance, always one of my favorites. Redemption. There needs to be a redemption story as clearly and profoundly presented as a tragedy. You start to think of that as you enter the second half of the sixth, no I guess it is the seventh decade of your life. You, young man, have a long time yet before that will be an issue for you." She laughed, but it was hollow.

He didn't join her laughing.

"*The Winter's Tale?*" He really seemed to be considering this revelation as of some importance. "Well, I had always thought I gave the choice of reflections for the days of aging to *King Lear* and *The Tempest* – it is interesting to see which actors choose to do which play. Of course, the supreme egoists want to do them both – but it takes a very different actor, man or woman, to be a grand Lear or a grand Prospero."

She was silent, thinking about what he had said, and how he'd said it. " It's hard to grow old. You spend too much time thinking. And Mac ... Mac is a great thinker. When I realized that he was depressed about Meggie's suicide I tried to divert him. I pushed the Little Globe activities. Theatre is versatile and uses the gifts of the person. We are talking kids here, or mostly kids. And he loved kids. This is what Mac loves – kids, Shakespeare and the parks, and maybe me. Kids in the Little Globe with just a simple bundle of props and silks, a crown, a flagon, take on a part – from overheard Bard or the playwriting of their own imaginations. Little toy ships re-create the storm in *Tempest* and in *Twelfth Night*; little horses, Agincourt. And above the doorway, in Mac's best gothic script, is a new line, misbegotten from its original, but fair use enough in this place. *'The play's the thing in which to catch the conscience ... of everyone!'*

'If we had the resources to implement more creative ideas with more plays, Mac could really make this a first rate enterprise rather than a shabby little ... " There was pride in her voice now. She sounded just as crazy as her husband. What was wrong with her? Gwynne shook herself like Romeo the beagle coming home from a long walk on a rainy night.

The young man looked at her almost shyly. "Belike I would surely care to take that ride, Mrs Macbeth. I've come quite a ways to see this place."

"He'll be back soon, I'm sure, but he'll have shut the machinery down. Here," she was actually losing her mind. "I will call and tell him I am bringing you down. It will do him good to show the Dark Ride to someone who wants to appreciate it. He's been discouraged lately, more than discouraged. Are you interested?"

"In faith, I would."

He would. She could tell. He looked delighted and enthusiastic. The cell phone went to voice mail but she decided to walk down anyway. Romeo anticipated them and was standing midway before them with his leash in his mouth. The old beagle did not like rides – automotive or amusement – but he liked even less being left behind.

She shrugged into her jacket but turned at the door. "I don't believe I asked your name?" He was quiet. "What's your name?"

"It's Will."

She stopped and looked at him.

He smiled self-consciously. "Yes, it's Will, which makes it a little odd that I am interested in all things Shakespeare, but then-"

"Our name is Macbeth." She finished for him, clipped Romeo on to his leash and opened the door. The young man followed her.

The wind cut through them with a promise that last night's fine powder of snow would be doubled like trouble by this evening's storm. She shivered. For all the human effort to light the solstice with Christmas festivities and Hanukkah, even Kwanzaa, and the craziness of New Year, it was like a tiny child tossing a pebble against an ocean of the dark. She carried a large flashlight that she didn't quite need yet but would keep them from falling on their return. Mac hadn't taken it, but then he rarely took this much time for mechanical checks or sentimental journeys.

Their house was not far from the back boundary of the park, formed by "O-yell-o's" big coaster. She always told their employees not to mention the unfortunate smothering death of Desdemona when upselling the attraction. (The teenagers found it cool; mothers of eight year olds did not). "O-yell-o" loomed above them with the employees' entrance underneath.

The gate was open. When Mac was doing his winter rounds, he rarely bothered to lock it behind him while he was inside. Though there were a lot of woods, they were not tiptoeing like Birnam Wood, and there was nothing of value to steal. Each ride, now dark, looked forlorn; each refreshment stand or "Carousing House" carefully secured. In the summer they were more careful after hours. Someone might be tempted to spend the night, sleeping rough, in the park. Mac had looked at her and his eyes crinkled up on the sides. They were faded now, too, from gazing into his dreams too long, but he smiled. When he was young, he had often been the last one chucked out of a park, and there were times security guards at Canobie Lake hadn't found him. But not even a boy with a heartless home would be tempted to make a den in Denmark, their house of mirrors, in December.

She held back so Will came level with her. It wasn't smart to let him trail behind. She realized she was gripping the heavy torch and the leather lead hard and purposefully relaxed her knuckles. "See over there," she said, "that's the Little Globe." The building was an unprepossessing huddle in the twilight. Only someone who knew already would recognize the steep doughnut shape, the outside painted to look like its illustrious predecessor.

"It's not open to the air at the top, is it?" Will asked, looking at it appreciatively.

"No, but there are two skylights. They can be covered for the movies. It gives the feeling of the original as a theatre space. It is a far cry from a serious reconstruction, like in London, but we're proud of it.

"Over there – I don't know if you can see it now – is 'The Tempest,' the water ride. It's our grandchildren's favorite." She smiled.

"Do your grandchildren have Shakespearean names as well as your children?"

"'No." she wondered exactly when she had told him her children's names. "Ben and his partner Peter's kids are Sarah and Markie. Duff and his Gemma are expecting a little sister for Aiden in three more months. Neither Miranda nor Harry have significant others, much less kids. The highlight of our summer is the children's visit. Sarah and Aiden, the older ones, treat the park as their own personal domain. We have to watch or they'll order paying customers out of line, on the rare days when there are lines, so they can get on whatever ride they want whenever they want it. Quite the entitlement – owning an entire amusement park – even a somewhat shabby one. We understand from their parents, that their teachers report some boastful behavior. As far away as California and Iowa respectively they can brag about their 'grandsires' theme park without worrying that any of their little friends will come to visit."

"They will not be forsworn in all their prating."

She laughed and joined the game, "Zounds, no!"

Most of the structures were boarded tightly against storm or squatter. The Ferris wheel, the park's other boundary marker, rose as the far end of the path, its outline fading quickly. Gwynne turned at a path jutting at right angles from the main street. She was unconsciously moving quickly. She jumped when he spoke:

"Come, seeling night, scarf up the tender eye of pitiful day; ... light thickens; and the crow makes wing to the rooky wood: Good things of day begin to droop and drowse; while night's black agents to their preys do rouse."

There was a transparent un-self-consciousness as he recited the lines, but they sent a deeper chill through her anyway.

"Here." The disguised door was for maintenance or exit rather than the marginally grander front entrance with its wait-room and scrolling quotations. Gwynne was relieved that some of the lights were on in the gift shop where they entered. It was so silent in the shrouded park she feared she'd missed Mac in the gloom.

Well, they had been missing one another for a long time.

"Have a quick look around while I try to find my husband." She tied Romeo to a permanent ring near his store dog-bed and he settled, grateful for rest after the exertion. Heavy plastic shrouded the merchandise. There were no visible daggers, but there was a sign for candy bloody fingers. The typical eye-of-newt witches brew packets were for sale, and there were pointed hats and capes. Comic books were visible through plastic covered shelves. The full Shakespeare, the stand-alone graphic version and several of the single plays in both formats were well-represented. The Scottish couple appealed to mind and stomach.

Will glanced around with apparent interest but kept coming. Having him behind her again made her feel edgy, but she'd come too far to ask him to leave. She opened a gate that gave on to the tunnel of the Dark Ride on the other side and then she heard a familiar words from the Scottish Play, clear and sharp and dark:

I have lived long enough: my way of life
Is fallen into the sear, the yellow leaf;
And that which should accompany old age,
As honor, love, obedience, troops of friends,
I must not look to have; but, in their stead,
Curses, not loud but deep, mouth-honor, breath,
Which the poor heart would fain deny, and dare not.

The passage wasn't in the canned dialogue. They didn't use Macbeth's lines when he is suddenly aware of the besieging Birnam Wood. And this wasn't Voice-over Doug, a theatre major at Emerson College so very proud of his first credit. These despairing words were in the voice of the man himself – not bloody thane, but kind and somewhat kooky teacher, her own strange bard-husband, as weary as she was herself of these many months of failing proceeds and a standing ovation of expenses.

"Mac!" she called more sharply than she intended. "Mac, where are you?" There was no answer, but she plunged ahead along the side of the track as far as possible from the electrified rail just in case it was live. She trembled. All her complaining of these afternoon hours became merely a ghost-dagger. The man who won her heart so long ago was everything to her. He wasn't going to ... he couldn't ... surely things were not so dire as all that. "Mac, please, where have you gone?"

"Pray pardon me. Let me go ahead." The young man slipped around her and nervous as she had been about his following her in the park earlier, she was grateful for his youth and agility now.

"You don't know the way! It sounds like he's nearly at the end of the Dark Ride. Near the platform that we use for dry ice now but where I played that one small scene. The place we kill Lady Macbeth or let her kill herself."

"Marry, I think it's pretty simple from here."

"Beware the electric rail!"

"In truth, I'll never mind it." he darted forward and she followed, losing him to sight but still hearing him ahead in the tunnel. Something was wrong. She was glad that their passing was not a big enough shadow to trigger the special effects – she didn't want to be surrounded by the weird-sister technology. She was huffing like a card-carrying AARP as she turned the last corner on the ride. The car was there and the illumination was the brightest in the tunnel.

Will called, "Lady, Mistress, do you have your cell phone? Call the EMTs. He's collapsed. Perchance his heart. It's beating, oh, it is beating very well, but he's unconscious."

By then, she'd reached him. She was shaking. She climbed in the car and gathered Mac up in her arms, hitching into her pocket for the phone. She got out the cell phone and handed it to Will. "You. Call. Now." She stared at him. "You know how, don't you?"

The young man paused, staring at it for a second as if processing information, then flicked it open and called.

"Is there an address here to give for 911 or ... will they know?"

"They will, Will." She wanted to laugh, to laugh hysterically but instead she clutched Mac as hard as ever she could. "Don't play the coward now, you crazy old Macbeth. I love you, damn it. Tempest and fairies and weird sisters and Shylock and Agincourt – you fool. You wonderful Jacques who promised that you would stay with me all the seven ages. Don't you dare leave me now or I will ... I will follow you into the grave and harrow you up to recite a sonnet to me once again."

He stirred just a little bit.

"Gwynnie?"

"Oh darling..."

He took a deep breath.

... Bare ruin'd choirs, where late the sweet birds sang.
In me thou seest the twilight of such day
As after sunset fadeth in the west ...

"Well ..." he took a deep breath, "that's all the sonnet I can recall."

She wanted to shake him – she absolutely wanted to shake the Shakespeare right out of him. Instead she eased his head into her lap. "If you have enough breath for that, I won't be quite so distraught, my love, but what you are doing in the Dark Ride in this dark night all alone I do not know."

"Do you love me in spite of all of this?" his voice was barely above a whisper.

It was what she had been thinking about all afternoon – whether she loved him in spite of all of this. Did he irritate her? Yes. Was she tempted to take a month's vacation someplace warm where they had never heard of Capulets or carousels? Yes. Could she imagine a life without him and his quotes and quibbles? Never. Where were the EMTs anyway? The park was not far from the firehouse. Dogberry stupid New Hampshire! Her husband was looking at her closely. She brushed a curling strand of dark but graying hair out of his eyes and whispered:

> ... *Love is not love*
> *Which alters when it alteration finds,*
> *Or bends with the remover to remove:*
> *O no! It is an ever fixed mark*
> *That looks on tempests and is never shaken;*
> *It is the star to every wandering bark*
> *Whose worth's unknown, although his height be taken.*
> *Love's not Time's fool, though rosy lips and cheeks*
> *Within his bending sickle's compass come:*
> *Love alters not with his brief hours and weeks,*
> *But bears it out, even to the edge of doom...*

"Let's not put you at the doors of doom just yet, my Orlando, my Orsino, my aggravating Prospero."

"Who's this?" he asked and for a moment she didn't know what he meant, and then she looked up to see the young man, holding out her cell phone. Mac struggled to sit up, to be more presentable, ever the showman. "How are you?"

How are you, you idiot, she thought, collapsed in a fun house tunnel wondering if you're meeting a paying customer. Oh, but her love could irritate her, he could. "This is Will..." she paused but the young man did not insert a surname and she went on. "He came this afternoon to see the park and said how much he would like to take the Dark Ride. We decided to come over and, if the ride were still live, perhaps he could take it. He's very interested in everything, in the park and the plays. He's studying...did you say you were studying?"

"Not exactly. It's more a life experience. I am pleased to meet you, Mr. Macbeth, and, from all I can see, it is a magnificent park."

"Well, we don't know how much longer-"

"Oh, but you must keep it open – it's wonderful! Nothing quite like it ever."

That was surely true. She looked at her husband's face, white and drawn. He would fight going to the hospital but he would not win. There were noises in the tunnel.

Will un-bent. "I'll go and lead them in."

"Don't let them break anything." Macbeth stirred as if he wanted to personally prevent any such disaster.

She held his head in her lap lovingly but firmly. "Anything broken we can fix."

Will was up and looked at them both. "I must away good gentles." And he was.

He obviously did a good job of directing the fire rescue squad into the attraction because they didn't break anything, and they found the Macbeths and extricated them from the car in the tunnel in spite of winking lights, dry ice fog, floating daggers and chanting witches – all of which their more hefty bulk and equipment triggered. The three would have stories to tell over Christmas dinners. It was one of the most interesting rescues they had ever performed. Still, given the possibilities, make-believe bloody hands were the kind they approved, and dead people that were only holograms were comforting.

One who'd slept through high school English and history saw various corpses in Scottish historical dress and wondered how ambulances transported folks with swords and boots like that. Mac told him to come back with his family – admission free. All of them must come. Next May, the park would be open again.

The rescue crew always maintained that they found their own way in. The side door was open, and they followed the lights and voices. No young man with a pointed beard was their guide. They had not seen anyone or a motorcycle (and the one who imagined ambulances on the heath would have noticed). Mrs. Macbeth had placed the 911 call herself. Hadn't she?

She didn't push the issue – just happy to be in the emergency room and happy once there to wait and wait and wait hours for

26

periodic five minute visits. It meant he was not a serious case. They kept him overnight, and she stayed past midnight, watching him as if he were a phantom to vanish as quickly and mysteriously as their visitor. She went back to their little cottage looking over her shoulder and wondering. In the morning when she pulled out the car to pick her husband up from the hospital she could see no motorcycle tracks in the snow at all.

But there was a second teacup. In fact, chiding herself for superstition, she took that cup unwashed and set it aside on a high shelf so that she could come back to it later and think about it some more.

Mac was released, given nitroglycerin to put under his tongue and told to watch his diet, take more regular exercise and eliminate worry. She would take care of the first two and was absolutely hopeless with the third one. Well, who's to care? They had passed the solstice. They had taken the Dark Ride and come from it wondrous well.

> *When in disgrace with fortune and men's eyes,*
> *I all alone beweep my outcast state,*
> *And trouble deaf Heaven with my bootless cries,*
> *And look upon myself, and curse my fate,*
> *Wishing me like to one more rich in hope,*
> *Featured like him, like him with friends possessed,*
> *Desiring this man's art, and that man's scope,*
> *With what I most enjoy contented least:*
> *Yet in these thoughts myself almost despising,*
> *Haply I think on thee, and then my state*
> *(Like to the lark at break of day arising*
> *From sullen earth) sings hymns at heaven's gate;*
> *For thy sweet love remembered such wealth brings*
> *That then I scorn to change my state with kings.*

She thought they could do less with the tragedies and more with the sonnets next season. Find a poets' group, host a reading or a summer institute. They could even hire someone, perchance an actor, to represent young Will Shakespeare himself to wander around the grounds listening to and approving all the little playlets in All the World's a Stage.

ENTER FRIAR, STAGE LEFT

Hold, daughter: I do spy a kind of hope,
Which craves as desperate an execution.
As that is desperate which we would prevent.
If, rather than to marry County Paris,
Thou hast the strength of will to slay thyself,
Then is it likely thou wilt undertake
A thing like death to chide away this shame ...
Romeo and Juliet

And she said "yes," of course. She was young. She was in love. It wasn't *Twilight* with the undead and the werewolves, but it was pretty overwhelmingly emotional. And he had the plan. Of course, he had the plan. He was the friar.

This time we tell the story, I am the friar.

Well, actually I'm the local minister and I have no business getting involved in the romances of the young. These are the *very* young. Me? My personal young and foolish romances have all grown old and bald long ago. I am no longer young. Foolish? You can judge for yourself.

Where be these enemies? Capulet! Montague!
See, what a scourge is laid upon your hate,
That heaven finds means to kill your joys with love.

That is the saddest story of all. For some reason it is on all the reading lists of teenagers. It doesn't deter them, of course. It should be on the reading list of parents. Maybe it should be in the seminary curriculum. For, yes, there is always a friar, or some kind of semi-religious or, at least, believe-in-hope-and-human-nature person in the background – one that says, "look, if you do this and this, maybe, just maybe, you can have your love in spite of all the hates between your people."

But wait – my story isn't told yet. It isn't yet friar-assisted suicide gone desperately wrong. It begins at the church caroling party where they meet and everything starts to go so very right and sparkly and full of maybe-happiness ... and only then so very wrong.

All these kids ... well, let me give you a cast list. It's the traditional way to do it when the play's the thing, and it may help you as they make their entrances.

Jess – she's our Juliet and has been a member of this little church longer than I've been pastor here. OK, that's only two years and things didn't end so well in my last parish. I am particularly motivated to stay here.

Jess was baptized here and told me that she's been caroling since she was five - she's gone to nursing homes, to shut-in elders in their homes, to the trailers of folks on the hospice list, who, by definition, will not see another Christmas. Like every teenage girl, she expects a future full of Christmases. Jess is at the pretty end of ordinary. Not gorgeous, but her smile lights up the room. In her senior year, she's ready to leave this town altogether – *really* ready. "No commitments in senior year," she announces. I've been a minister long enough to practically smell famous last words.

That's Jess. Now you need to know about her circle. Tim is her cousin. Big mouth. Vain. Supremely engaged with fashion but, no, not gay. If he imagines someone looking at him cross-eyed, he gets aggressive. Not a church-member here or anywhere else except maybe Our Lady of the Mirror, Tybalt – I mean Tim – was at caroling as court-ordered community service. As a favor to Jess, I said I would sign off on him.

Patrick O'Leary. He's in love with Jess. Did I mention her

"no strings because we are all heading to college" policy? Patrick is the reason for that season. Patrick's the son of Jess's dad's CEO, and it would be convenient for the parents if the kids "hooked up" (a direct quote from Jess' mother) or at least she did not snub him. Honestly Cap and Joan would probably be fine if Jess would just go with Patrick to the Winter Formal. "Is that too much for parents to ask?" says Joan at coffee hour.

Seriously? Have they forgotten what it was like to be eighteen and have parents suggest a date for a dance? Much less use the words "hook up" without exactly knowing what it means? Probably if Dad just said, look, this would help me out and you never have to see him again, she'd groan and go. Jess is that sweet a kid. But Mom tells people the two are "a couple." Quarterback on the football team and goalie in hockey, grades decent and he wants to go into business. Perfect, right?

I'm amazed Jess gives Patrick the time of day. Him? He doesn't recognize the brush off when the bristles hit him. So, Roman Catholic or not, he shows up for youth group. At this liberal Protestant church, we are happy for any warm body – no zombie allusions intended. And probably zombies, too, at least the emergent still-speaking kind.

Back to "friends" of Jess. Tim, not really. Patrick, even less. Anne Bailey actually shouldn't be in that category either. Anne is ten years older than the rest of the kids, Jess' babysitter when Jess was little. Jess's parents – two careers, two social lives, no time for their only child. Anne took over from the nanny after Jess went to first grade, coming every afternoon, usually making her supper, often helping with her bath, reading her stories. They were sixteen and six, then seventeen and seven and so on. The confidences went both ways, the playing, the favorite television shows. At some point Jess may have actually become more mature than Anne.

Anne doesn't have much going on at the advanced age of twenty-eight. She lives through Jess's high school life, probably not good for either of them, but Jess's parents are thrilled to have a built-in nurse, I mean, chaperone. They still don't see much of their only child. They expect more. See Patrick above.

Madison Rose is gorgeous. Everybody turns around to look at Madison Rose, guys and girls. Jess's best friend. Take a boyfriend, please says M.R., happy to share. She would even donate to Anne! Take them all! That's the secret. Madison Rose doesn't like guys, but she's nobody's stereotype of a lesbian. For good or bad, stereotype is the coin of the realm in this small town, so no one sees it. Look at me. No, it's not about me.

OK that's Capulets. How about Montagues? Let me introduce Rashid Mahmood, our Romeo. Wait, one more digression. Let me explain just a little bit more about this very liberal church. They like their liberal, they are proud of it, as long as the challenge isn't too deep. A Muslim coming to youth group is not a negative (especially since there are only two Muslim families in town). It's an "interfaith opportunity." In fact, you would think that everyone would be excited about extravagant hospitality. And they are – youth, church council, missions committee. Everyone except the Carsons. Jess's uncle died in the World Trade Center on September 11, 2001.

Does it even matter to Cap and Joan what Rashid is like as a human being?

Cap Carson is a deacon (though he rarely spares the time for meetings). In the past he said that youth group was a community gift. This year he suggested it be closed to those of other faiths. I assure you he does not mean Roman Catholic; he does not mean Patrick. He does not, in fact, mean Jewish. Joan has two Jewish brothers-in-law. By "other faiths" he means these relatively new Muslim kids in town. Cap packages everything together – from al-Qaeda to the Boston Marathon bombing, new terrorists in Syria and Iraq, every Fox News suspicion – and lays it on thin teenaged shoulders.

Two years into my ministry here and twenty-two months past the new-pastor honeymoon (you do the math) and I took my first stand.

Jesus, I've got to stand somewhere.

Of course, how'd that work for him?

Anyway Rashid. Dreamy (honestly, even I think so). Dreamy looks, but probably reads-too-much-Rumi dreamy, too, if you know what I mean. Tall, thin, huge brown eyes. He lives with his Palestinian grandmother, parents and twin sisters. They are Egyptian on his father's side of the family. Very excited about the original hopes of the Arab spring. Worried about everything Mideast since that time. Rashid is likely to be valedictorian. Fencing is his only sport. Did I mention that Jess has been known to occasionally play Uno, but wouldn't know a first down if her pillow were stuffed with it? Fencing? She knows it is not about horseback riding and barbed wire, but just.

But is Rashid interested in Jess? Not at all. Rashid is madly in love with Madison Rose. That's also in the category of famous last words ... or famous last kisses, though he admits that he's never kissed Madison Rose. He does write poetry about her mouth. And Madison Mahmood has beautiful alliteration, he thinks. He is kidding, right? Actually it was her Rose middle name that made me first realize we just tripped on to the stage right in the middle of *that* play.

When the play opens we meet Romeo, the original Romeo, breaking up a fight between his friends and the Capulets and going on about how he is in love with Rosaline. In *Romeo and Juliet* she never appears. She's in the wings, but you know that she's gorgeous, and Romeo is that guy, the one who loves the girl from afar, who "dreams" about living a life of devotion. Rashid, too, is that guy – in love with love. It gets everyone in trouble, every time. Love!

Montagues. Mahmoods. Rashid's friends. Ben and Rashid are cousins. Ben's family is more Americanized – get this – Ben Mann. You look at him and wonder, who do you think you're fooling? But his girlfriend, not an intellectual whiz, a girl named Jazmin told her friends, who told their friends, one of whom told me because I am the friar and I always hear last, that her boyfriend with the dark eyes and curly black hair – so yummy, (yes, she said "yummy") oh, yes, and he is Italian! And – big secret, hush, hush – they changed their name when they emigrated. Benvolio, of course. His real last name is "something," says she with a straight face, "something like manicotti."

I could not make this up.

Ben was born Behnam. Ben's fine with Ben. Not ethnic-proud, not ethnic-shy. Likes girls, golf and computers in that order, although he thinks he is most likely to make a living from the computers. Does not like to fight and tries to get Rashid as far away from any kind of conflict as possible. Conflict happens. I don't think I mentioned yet that Rashid has very strong feelings about Israel. Yes. His grandma lost all her children except Rashid's mom when a bomb hit their house in the Gaza strip. So he gets pretty worked up about Palestinian issues.

Now Matt. What can I say about Matt? Rashid's best friend. Not an immigrant, except in the way that everyone is an immigrant to the Abenakis. Son and grandson of a selectman and in this town you become a selectperson (I've only met the male version – I have it on the best authority that the early 1990s saw a selectwoman) if you are generations in the town, and have not lived, even briefly, in the adjacent town.

Matt. He's full of imagination, wit, satire, even. Mercurial. He broods and he flashes, loves to play with verbal sexual double meanings. Love is sex, in his not-so-humble opinion, though he knows better than to try to convince Rashid. He is already a freshman in college, but lives at home. See above about not moving away. He is hotheaded, and cannot stand anyone who is affected or pretentious or focused on fashion. Does that sound like anyone? Oh, right. Tim. Got it in one.

Thas is a sophomore in high school. He follows Rashid around like a puppy. He's a garden variety Protestant kid, American several generations without being Mayflower. However, the hero worship of Rashid affects him so that he will tell you that when he is old enough he is going to change his name to Ahmed. Thas worries about his complexion and is just a little chubby. He has a few self-image problems.

There are other youth group kids. Sam, Greg and Aiden, Gin, Sophie. Different ones come different weeks. Like most teenagers, friends by convenience, they side with the clique they guess will be popular tomorrow. Whatever. I don't judge. A lot of adults work on that level all their lives. They teach it to their children.

Cast of characters. I've lingered. You've figured out I'm trying to put off the play. You see I'm clergy. I love my work. When it comes to scripts like this, I fancy myself the playwright. Maybe stage manager. Not a bit part. Or a bitter one. But in this show I am the Friar.

Character sketch of me? Lawrence (not Larry, please) Brothers. Thirty-five and ordained seven years. Gay, not married. Looking, but it is really, really, really difficult in a small parish. The misconduct guidelines are strict and that means I can't date anyone in a twenty-five mile radius who might ever even come to a wedding, funeral or Fourth of July parade (where I play sax on a float while the choir sings "When the Saints Go Marching In" over and over and over again). In fact, I think the church (I was out to the Search committee, of course, after the last fiasco) would really prefer that I go to Boston gay bars rather than fall in love, get married, and have a couple kids. They tell me they do not want *Modern Family* in their parsonage. Well, I'm tempted to tell them I wasn't expecting the vestry from *Vicar of Dibley* either.

Other information about me? I love lovers. I have a soft heart for lovers whose situation doesn't fit what people around them want. And I am (too much I guess) always the kind of person with a plan. Oh, I am also really into herbs. No, don't jump ahead. You would be wrong, but, truly, my deck is all about the herb pots and more than just mint and basil – I love experimenting.

I wanted to experiment with my second Advent. Not herbally – liturgically. I wanted something new. A live nativity, you know, with animals. A pageant by adults for kids rather than the other way around. Caroling for homeless shelters instead of nursing homes and hospice patients. A different kind of Christmas Eve service ... maybe at midnight. How not-too-out-of-the-gift-box is that? But the deacons were clear. No experiments at all. Everything the way it always is. But, friends, that can't happen and the new thing this year was tragedy.

So Scene 1, I guess ... well, Act 1, Scene 1. December. Dark at four. Burglar prevention lights in the parking lot so it looks like noon. The kids are early. I shut my laptop, wave vaguely at the returning singers, head for the kitchen. The caroling after-party is my responsibility. Cocoa, cookies, popcorn, music and some stupid DVD – *Elf* or *Christmas Story* or *Bad Santa*. It makes the popcorn logical.

They all pile out of their cars. Jess gets out of the same car as Madison Rose, Anne's old Saturn. Rashid is with Ben and Matt in Bill Cooley's Prius. He's our Mission Committee Palestinian issues activist, with a bumper sticker that reads, "Jesus is born in Bethlehem every year." The chaperones, except for Anne, lay their fingers aside of their respective noses and disappear like Saint Nick. Sam and Greg are being loud and obnoxious, one-upping each other with jokes about people with developmental delays, same-gender loving couples, and Middle Easterners (those were not any of the nouns they used). Ben, as always is peacemaker.

"Hey, guys. Enough with that. Who wants to help me get the popcorn started?"

"Hey rag-head – don't think you want any of our church popcorn. It's made really tasty by being cooked in *pork oil!*" That's Sam, never much for creativity.

"Give it a rest. I think you strained your brain with 'Silent Night.'"

"Yeah, well, your singing it hurt baby Jesus' feelings."

"I suppose you don't know that Muslims respect Jesus and there is much about his mother Mary in the Qu'ran."

Patrick comes in hitching up those low-slung pants, which must look attractive on someone. "Shut up about the Virgin Mary. She's the Queen of Heaven. My grandmother has a statue in her bedroom and it tells her when someone she knows is going to die."

Matt's usually too smart for this, but it must have been the dim of the moon. "Your grandma's statue tells her what numbers to play."

Patrick turns red but doesn't seem to be able to find any words. A frequent problem, usually leading to fists.

Tim wades in. (Mind you I'm not there for any of this. It is all hearsay and teenage hearsay at that.) The pants look good on Tim and the shoes cost two hundred dollars and his hair is cut and gelled like he thinks he's not Team Jacob but the real deal. He has a cup of designer coffee. He skipped the last house and hit the strip mall, mumbling that cocoa, like Trix, is for kids.

"Hey, you guys! Think you should be here? I hear some Navy Seals might be stopping by real soon."

Rashid is still craning around for a glimpse of Madison Rose and not paying any attention. It's Matt, offended on their behalf and pretty much embarrassed for the whole Christian religion as represented by Tim and Patrick, who swings the punch. It doesn't connect with Tim's jaw or anything really satisfying but it knocks the latte up and out of his hands and splashes Tim with coffee from head to foot. He freaks.

"You son of a bitch! You miserable small town moron. I'm going to break your friggin' ..."

"Tim! Shut up now!" Jess is there.

We are still talking parking lot, right? I was happy and oblivious, upending bags of cookies on trays, scanning ancient DVD cases for holiday fare. Maybe this less-than-Christian verbal repartee would not have happened if I were there. Perhaps I flatter myself. By the time it escalates to smack-and-splash I'm probably doing something with salsa and replacing the Five Hour Energy one of the kids brought with Mountain Dew. That's as high-test as they get from me.

Jess is present. Very present. She is fierce and beautiful in the moment. All of five foot four, she storms up right under her cousin's nose and says very, very quietly. "Leave right now. I don't care where you go and I also honestly don't care ..." she looks at him with supreme disdain, "... if you ever get the stains out of your fancy fleecy-weecy. In fact, I don't care if Santa puts coal in your stocking or if I ever see you again. Go *right now*."

And he does, trying to retain shreds of coffee-stained dignity. His fabulous little BMW contrasts with the other kids' pre-owns. He slams the door and guns the motor like a two year old in a tantrum, spins gravel and ice and is gone. Jess glances toward Patrick and then looks right through him.

She notices Matt. "Shattuck, did you sing your *brains* out, or do the twelve days of Christmas just make you as dumb as whoville?"

She walks over to Ben but includes Rashid vaguely in her reconciliation. "I am so sorry about my cousin. He's clueless and ... well, I'm really glad you joined us for caroling. Uh ... " she has to know why the boys are there – it is, after all, a very small town, "Maddy-Rose has already gone home, She had a huge test to study for ... I hope you are still coming in for the party. I personally would be really pleased."

She is hesitant. She is earnest. She has a tiny scar at the corner of her mouth from the time she fell off her bike at eight years old. It gives her a very little bit of smile even when she's being serious and Rashid thinks that it would be very sweet to kiss.

He is undone.

It is and ever has been the way of Romeos in every generation. *"See, how she leans her cheek upon her hand! O that I were a ... glove upon that hand, that I might touch that cheek!"* The only update necessary with the years? He's thinking "mitten."

"Oh, yes, I'd love to come in. Sure. I'm looking forward to it. No offense taken. Your cousin is just well ..." Yes, it is a small town and he also knows her family's sensitivity. "Look, I can understand anyone in your family being a little anxious about Muslims, so we can cut him some slack, right guys?" The gentle little punch in Ben's triceps will leave a bruise. As for Matt, Rashid makes a poniard with his eyes and pins him. "We are not offended. Love some ... cocoa, ... cheese puffs ...?"

"Popcorn."

They wince, then smile, then laugh. "Definitely, popcorn. Come on Matt, Ben, Thas?"

This last dialogue of scene 1 is not hearsay. Jazmin came running in the church and said the guys were going to fight in the parking lot and I had to do something ... please. I always thought she was the dimmest bulb on the tree but maybe not. I witness this interchange and so I actually see the *a rose by any other name would smell as sweet* happening right before my eyes. He is fully aware. She is not. She does have an unfocused look around her eyes and drifts into the church. It is not lost on Anne, however, and Anne has never left a thought unspoken, so I hear this, as I trail behind the two girls. "Jess? Jess! OMG he's so sweet. And he likes you. Seriously. He's a doll – I'm totally looking him up on Facebook ..."

I guess this is Act 1, Scene 2.

As they say, immediately after the preceding.

Pause for Smartphone. Jess is still drifting, hasn't said anything. Anne's thumb and first finger are making like baby birds. Worried, but happy for her young alter ego.

Rashid in the meantime is in the kitchen helping with everything like ADD – A boy Deep with Drama. The snacks. The hot-air popper. Did I need help with the cocoa? Hey, Thas, lend a hand with these chairs.

Tim has, of course, departed, but Patrick is here. And who also has his Smartphone out? You guessed it, and from what happens shortly I am guessing that he is the one who called the Carson's house. In about fifteen minutes "we-are-so-very-busy" has time to pick up her daughter.

Meanwhile Anne has chasing-hashtags across her face. Jess is watching Rashid. Matt leans against the counter with his eyes in a tennis match from one to the other, openly laughing, and Ben is fending off Jazmin's super attentive attentions to see if he is wounded. Since he was three feet from the physical aggressor and the level of combat did not escalate above Starbucks cup, of course, he is not wounded. But then he does something male and stupid like leave-me-alone and her big blue eyes brighten up with tears and she sulks and then he follows her somewhere because he has hurt her feelings. He, at least, is not an Arab presence when Joan Carson pulls up in the regulation Mom SUV to collect her daughter.

"Mom, the party hasn't even started!"

"You have a pile of homework sitting in your room at home, darling. I think you said you were not going to stay for the party."

"I changed my mind. It's going to be fun and Rev. Lawrence needs my help."

I barge in. I can't help it. There is not a pastor in the world who doesn't love having capital Love happening inside the church where usually everything is blandly Friendly or Tolerant or, well, let's face it Hypocritical.

"Jess is a huge help. I'll give her a lift home if you'd like, Joan."

Flash freeze. Her eyes. My body. Joan Carson is a pro.

As if I had not said anything. As if I did not exist.

"Jess, your Dad and I want to talk with you about a little plan we have for a cruise in January. Very exciting – St. Thomas. I know you will want to hear all about it."

"Anne can give me a ride later. Sure, I'd love to know about your trip."

"*Our* trip ... our trip as *a whole family*! A little pre-graduation reward for somebody who got early admission to Brown. Pretty special, darling."

"Oh, my. Thanks, Mom."

I wonder from her expression whether Jess has ever been on

a vacation with good old Mom and Dad. This parental taser obviously stuns her, but the original and major stun is still her heightened awareness of Rashid. I know and she knows, probably the most clueless teenager at the party, and certainly Joan Carson knows that Jess does not want to leave the church. She would like very much to do some on-site research into what these new feelings are. However, it doesn't look like she has a choice.

"I'll get my things. Bye guys, see you in school tomorrow." She gives the room a general nod. Things are moving along. Joan has given Patrick a quick smile, confirming my suspicion, but it is Matt, whose family is socially prominent enough that he cannot be ignored, who actually pushes himself away from the counter and comes over to talk with her. Or rather distract her.

As they chat, Jess vanishes. And Rashid vanishes. I find a job for Patrick, because already I am mixed up in the lives of these kids in ways that I should not be. I don't know how sorry I'll be. It's in the future and, God forgive me, I do not see it coming at all.

Jess and Rashid are gone for about fifteen minutes. Joan is tapping her lovely fingernails. Jess comes back into the hall alone – she's not completely stupid – looking a little deer-in-the-headlights, and whatever has been happening in the chilly sanctuary it involved some *Good night, good night! Parting is such sweet sorrow that I shall say goodnight till it be morrow.*

Act 2. Scene 1. In the choir loft. Several days later.

Rashid says, "*If I profane with my unworthiest hand this holy shrine, the gentle fine is this: My lips, two blushing pilgrims, ready stand to smooth that rough touch with a tender kiss.*"

Well, no. But, yes, more or less.

And Jess says, "*Good pilgrim, you do wrong your hand too much, which mannerly devotion shows in this; for saints have hands that pilgrims' hands do touch, and palm to palm is holy palmers' kiss.*"

In other words -- hold my hand, you dimwit.

"*Ay, pilgrim, lips that they must use in prayer.*"

41

About the right length for a tweet.

Rashid continues, *"O, then, dear saint, let lips do what hands do; They pray, grant thou, lest faith turn to despair."*

And this, I guess, is the direct result of a courtship begun in a church parking lot.

"Saints do not move, though grant for prayers' sake."

I am calmly writing my sermon in my comfortable office. The choir loft is icy, but I am pretty sure they do not feel the temperature.

"Then move not, while my prayer's effect I take. Thus from my lips, by yours, my sin is purged."

The people who put *Romeo and Juliet* on sophomore reading lists have a lot to answer for – not to speak of the teachers who still use memorization as a teaching tool. These seniors should be on to *Hamlet,* but see how much they remember when the play discovers them. Wish it worked in church, but every Christmas I ask encouragingly, "Who remembers from last year what the angels sing?" And the third graders sit, uneasy and without answer, like small silent reproaches that there's not been much "peace on earth" in their young lifetimes. But that's another story.

One good thing about a December romance is that the teachers are not expecting much from their students anyway. They certainly are not getting all-around academic effort from these two, though their Bard research is exemplary.

Jess says, *"Then have my lips the sin that they have took."*

Rashid, *"Sin from thy lips? O trespass sweetly urged! Give me my sin again."*

And it has nothing to do with study group. Nope I am sure about that, but she concludes, *"You kiss by the book."*

Which is when I arrive in the choir loft to grab a copy of next week's anthem. They hold up their well-thumbed copies of the Bard. Between them there is not much remorse. Actually, between them there are not many inches.

"Study date? Hmm. You'll have that Shakespeare down ... cold. Let's head to the kitchen. It's warming up for the homeless supper tonight. Cup of coffee, cocoa?"

Wasn't I just this age? caught just like this? and a more dangerous catching that, and more disastrous to home harmony, or so it seemed at the time. As teenagers we fear the world revolves around us. Now I feel a hundred and ten years old.

I don't quiz them. We talk of other things. I don't ask about their families. We talk politics – how the physician-assisted suicide bill everyone expected would pass the neighboring Massachusetts electorate was soundly defeated.

Act 2. Scene 2.

So, let me just tell you that in the real living of it, love is not, of course, as telescoped as it appears to be in a Shakespeare play. But damn close. I was happily oblivious to most of the teen drama that took place over the next couple weeks. There is quite enough going on in church in Advent – the mitten tree, the Blue Christmas service, the extra choir rehearsals, the children's pageant with parents to wrangle, not to speak of locating bathrobes and tinfoil crowns, shepherd burlap and crooks and bales of straw.

I'm guessing there was much romance – cyber and otherwise. Probably a number of *it is in the moon – no it's the sun* dialogues. Where they were able to get away to have time together at night is a mystery to me. If it was in a freezing-cold pew I would prefer to be the last person to know.

It's Tuesday and we are getting ready for the Christmas Tea. This is an afternoon event for older parishioners since they don't come out at night and night comes early this time of year. Peer Grietsen conducts all the regional school musical events and he brings a small choral group of young people each year to be the entertainment. The drinkers of tea from our (once-a-year polished) silver tea service donate generously to the spring chorus trip. Peer this year has brought twelve young men. Jackpot for these ladies. It doesn't matter whether they sing well. But they do. Classical, some silly, one Hanukkah song to prove they are a public school group.

43

Rashid has a solo, Mariah Carey's "All I Want for Christmas is You," and every woman in the room feels like he is singing to her. He isn't. Do they know who is the object of his affection? Of course not, but then again, they have probably not ever heard this song. These are "White Christmas" folks! Somehow they feel the genuineness of his emotion.

Rashid excuses himself to get some water and Peer leads the sing-along carols. Jess is washing serving plates and some teacups. She doesn't realize he's in the kitchen with her at first and so he gets a long unobserved look at her.

The air is suddenly so charged with disapproval it makes her look up.

"What have you done?" he's out of breath, not from singing.

"Do you like it?" She puts a finger tentatively up to the HijabGirl Lycra Blend Farah Silky Al-Amira Hijab. It's light blue. She bought it on Amazon.

"How dare you make fun of my faith?" Loud carols in the background.

Her tears start silently. "I'm not. I'm not making ... I was trying to ... to ... to show you how much ..."

"How much what? How much you can appropriate something that is definitive of women in my culture? Something my mother wears. My grandmother wears. Do you know anything about it – the tradition? My cousin Fatima does not wear a hijab and she is proud for her hair to show in public. It means something to wear it or not wear it. It is what gets Arab American girls bullied. It's not a fucking fashion accessory!" Rashid turns and it looks like he will storm back through the door altogether.

Jess is faster. She grabs his sleeve and pulls and there's a minute of sheer Shakespearean comic tug of war. She holds on and finally Rashid faces her. And waits.

"You know my family is the most anti-Arab family in town. I wanted to show you that I am not ... them. I am willing to change. I will go with you anywhere. I will learn to be who you want me to be. I'm sorry. I'm so sorry. Just show me how to do it right."

The anger deflates out of him in a big breath. "I don't need you, Jess, in a powder blue hijab. I need you to be you. I need Jess. I want Jess. Jess as Jess. Not your looks and not your family. You know my family isn't going to be any better with this than yours and the hijab would not make it any easier for them." He gently pulls it off her head. "There. There you are – there's my Jess. Not hiding."

"I'll never hide from you."

They kiss for a long time. He takes his thumb and wipes the tears off her cheek and kisses along their tracks. Finally she pushes him back and crooks that wicked dark eyebrow. "If you think hijabs are *not* a fashion accessory, my love, then you have never been on the Internet. Ever. These days they are not buying your grandma's hijab. I actually wanted the burgundy with the rhinestones."

He looks ... uninformed.

Act 2. Scene 3.

My sixty-two year old mother wears a dental-guard. She has it to keep her from grinding her teeth while she is sleeping, mostly having bad dreams about me. Once it was about my choice of lovers. Now it's my lack of same, and the subsequent delay in my adopting a grandchild. I do not remember promising this, but she is absolutely sure I did. Her memory is still fine, thank you.

So consider my surprise when the dentist tells me that I need a dental guard because I am "bruxing," destroying my teeth. Let's face it – the look of my mouth is important in my profession. So this tells me that I am taking other people's stressful lives way, way too seriously. It's not my life. Anyone who knows me, including my mother, will tell you -- I need to get one.

I suggest Ogunquit to the two young lovers. I've had many happy vacations in Maine and Ogunquit's only an hour's drive. Rashid and Jess want to walk, talk, avoid any chance of seeing people they know. I suggest a walk along the Marginal Way, bundled up like

... well, haven't I been listening to too much "Chestnuts Roasting on an Open Fire?"

I mean Saturday or after school. I do not mean they should play hooky today. That is what's wrong with us adults. We say things and then we expect that teenagers are going to hear the subtext of caution and reason. Not so much.

Jess and Rashid skip school. They drive off in separate cars. I imagine they stop somewhere and one car drives on. My imagination is working full tilt. Actually this scene is pieced together from things I later learned, but the truth is close to what I was imagining while it was taking place.

Walking the path high above the Atlantic Ocean – the surf is boiling up in foam. Occasionally a dog walker passes them going in the other direction.

"What do you think of New England?"

"I was little when I came here. My family is here. My friends. It's beautiful. You are asking me if I want to stay here?"

"I guess so," she drags a long strand of hair out of her eyes and mouth, twists it behind her ear and pulls her wool cap down more securely against the wind. She looks adorable, and very young.

She takes his breath away. Somehow he can still speak. "I always wanted to travel, my love. I wanted to live in the Middle East for a while, at least study there, perhaps the University of Beirut. I used to think I wanted to move to the southwest, Arizona or New Mexico, but feelings about immigrants are running so high there, I'm not sure anymore. Maybe California. Alaska would be fascinating. Imagine an Arab in Alaska. But everything is different now. Now I want to be where you are. You are a child of New England. It is beautiful because of you. Apple orchards, old stone walls and pine trees. Our children can make snow castles in the winter and sand castles in the summer."

She stops still, leaning to stay upright against the wind. "I am so relieved. I am so glad. Oh, Rashid. I was so afraid that you would want to stay here. I can't *wait* to leave. I want to see everything in the whole world, but only if I can see it with you. But I thought that maybe you had come here as a haven and would want to stay."

"You'll come with me?"

"Anywhere. Or everywhere. Let's go everywhere."

"Everywhere. Together." He pauses. It feels like a long time. The gulls cry and drop shells on to the rocks to break their breakfasts.

"I did not want you to wear a hijab."

"No." Jess replies in a small voice.

"But there is a custom from my country I would like to ... share."

He pauses so long that she looks up wondering.

"Engagement bands began in ancient Egypt. Really they did. Hush, dear, listen. The tradition is that the circle symbolizes a never-ending bond and that the space in the middle is a kind of entrance way."

He stops and takes her hand. Her left hand. He looks down at it. She is looking out to sea as if she expects a whale to breach and it is very important that she see it. She is not looking at her hand.

"An engagement ring is worn on the third finger of the left hand and this too has its source in ancient Egyptian myth that this finger contains a vein leading directly to the heart. Well, or maybe it's just because the heart is on the left side of the body."

"Yes," she says, very quietly.

Did they have a balcony scene? Maybe. I don't know. Did they have a wedding? Funny you should ask me.

Act 3. Scene 1.

It is Christmas Eve. The kid-friendly service at four o'clock is finished. It has battery operated LED tea lights instead of candles, a pageant, candy canes for everyone in honor of the shepherd's crooks, because symbols are important. The kid-friendly packs the church with all ages because it gives people the evening free to connect with different blendings of family and it makes them all feel like children once again. Jess reads the passage about the shepherds and the angels out in the fields. Shepherds are outcasts, I tell her. Think like an outcast when you read. She doesn't seem to have a problem with that. Forbidden love. Is that why these two kids matter so very much to me?

I like to have teens involved with younger children's activities. It demonstrates that big kids still like church and don't *all* vanish the moment their parents allow it. If I were just coming to one service, instead of working, this would be the one I'd attend. I don't even have kids (yet), but I want my "Silent Night" a little off-key, a little angels-poking-each-other. Rough, like it was. Not polished like a performance. The late-night service has dignified deacons proclaiming the lessons and the singing of carols with the oldest non-gender-inclusive lyrics possible, but honestly, that service is all about the choir – let us not beat around the music stand.

So, I'm in my office with my shoes off, feet on the desk, and well, I'm just resting my eyes. In a few minutes I'll decide whether to bring communion to the hospital tonight or tomorrow. Both Christmas Eve and Christmas Day are lousy times to be in the hospital, tied to an IV pole while piped in music plays "There's No Place like Home for the Holidays." A soft tap on the office door, ah, wakes me. I swing the feet down and behind the desk. No time to put on the shoes.

"Come in." I say it with as much Ho-Ho and as little Grinch as I have available. Jess comes around the door, with a small secret smile that does not require her little scar to turn up her lips. Earlier she was wearing a deep green handmade cable knit sweater (she is definitely in the teenage knit and crochet crowd) for the service with black slacks and a green and black Serrv scarf from Indonesia. Very lovely and she was seasonal without any little bell earrings. I notice clothes. I like clothes.

Now she is stunning in a creamy white sweater, boat neck with sequins sewn in and a midcalf skirt one shade darker. Latte, maybe. Her hair sweeps up and there is a wreath of silver accented with crimson berries lightly lying on her hair. She is wearing more makeup than I've seen on her, but it isn't little-girl-playing dress-up. It's beautiful. I realize what she wants just by looking at her.

"Pastor Lawrence, will you marry us?"

My toes hunt frantically and unsuccessfully for my shoes. I give up.

"Come on in, Jess. I don't suppose you are alone. It takes two to get married." I go around the desk stocking-footed and motion them to the little circle of chairs. She sits and I reach out and shake Rashid's hand. Black corduroy slacks and a charcoal sweater with a pearl gray shirt and ... yes ... a bright red tie to match her berries. Before he shakes my hand he transfers a ring box into his left hand.

Instinctively I glance down. The third finger on Jess' left hand is lit by a ruby surrounded by diamond chips.

I sigh, and see from their disappointed faces that they hoped for a happier response, so I smile. It's genuine. It's just that I know, even then, how hard it's going to be. At least I think I know.

"Congratulations, Jess, Rashid. I am happy at your engagement. I was sighing because this is not going to be easy for you. You're young. You have plans for next year ... and your families, well ... it's going to be a lot to explain."

I hear myself and I know I sound like the marriage is a done deal. A better minister or maybe a different minister might have started off trying to dissuade them. Not me. They are sure enough and just old enough that it's going to happen here or at a justice of the peace and, at least, here there will be some heavy-duty praying, which they are going to need. However, I do plunge into delay-the-day tactics.

"Usually when couples are engaged they come for a series of visits – we make plans, discuss their compatibility, and talk through ceremony choices. Shortest time frame is probably three months and some couples take as much as two years. In your case a longer time might give your families a chance to become comfortable with your choice of partner and with getting married at a young age ... they might realize you are responsible enough ..." I drifted off.

Jess is shaking her head very firmly. "We want to get married tonight."

"You have a license?" Why did I ask? What was I thinking?

"Of course, we do." Rashid replies, as if I have accused him of still riding a tricycle. "All is in order, even the wedding bands." He clutches the box a little more tightly. For witnesses we have Madison Rose and Matt. They are in the narthex. Actually I think they are cleaning up bulletins and stuff from the four o'clock service."

"Of course they are." I inhale. Exhale. "You've only known each other a few weeks."

"We've been in school together for several years now. We weren't strangers the night of the caroling party." Jess is arguing. Rashid simply gazes at her.

I try again. "Can we take two more weeks and think about this?"

"No." she is firm. "In January my parents plan to take me on a cruise. I'm not going. It's their combination kidnap, bribe, exile plan. They want keep me away from Rashid and I would not put anything ... *anything* past them. I have my college acceptance now – we can move to Providence. Rashid and I will get jobs and Rashid will apply to schools there. I'm going to be to be with Rashid."

She inherited her mother's organize-the-garden-club gene.

"Don't you think your parents want to be part of a wedding? Every mother of the bride wants a part in organizing a wedding, however intimate, and certainly, Rashid, your parents would like to be here. Your grandmother ..."

"My parents won't set foot in a church. My grandmother will probably go into mourning for me when she discovers that I have married a woman whose mother has Jewish connections and whose father is Christian."

I wince. I look at Jess. She looks back. "My parents will be even less happy than that, trust me. They will get a lawyer to try to undo the wedding."

She takes a deep breath. Does she know these are fighting words for me?

"Trust me, my mother gets her own way. And this is the woman who hasn't noticed my existence for years, who did not attend the school play last month. I had the lead. Or any other play I've been in. What about girl scouts, T-ball, Middle School Chorus, Brownies, or any Christmas pageant ever? Nope. Too busy. All of a sudden she's oh-so-interested in every little thing I do. A latent paranormal maternal sense has surfaced and she suspects everything. I should have tried falling in love younger when I was desperate to be on her radar!" Jess takes another gulping breath.

"And ..."

"We are not going to tell them right away. We are leaving two weeks from now. We promise not to scare them but we won't tell them where we are."

"Jess!" My voice is sharp. "Don't want to know. What about school? You have to finish off high school."

They have not thought of that. They're eighteen? Oh, they're eighteen. I see the way their eyes meet and I can feel them brain-tweeting. I'm not sure if I'm pleased or angry at myself for dimming their shine.

Rashid speaks quietly. "We will make arrangements. I only actually need one class to graduate. Jess ...?"

"Two classes. We can take them at a community college. That's a perfect reason to keep our marriage secret for a few weeks until the arrangements are made ..."

"Why don't you keep on planning, but hold off the wedding until ..."

"No!" it's Jess. She looks suspicious. She should be. She should have a reason to be suspicious of me, but, in fact, she doesn't. I want to have a partner I can look at the way she looks at Rashid.

"I won't tell anyone. I promise. I just think you need more time."

I won't. I do. They do.

"We are getting married tonight. I want it very specifically to be Christmas Eve that we are married. For the sake of the ... baby."

There is a pause. I don't ask – which baby is that? Probably not Jesus.

Rashid leans forward. He's notices my stocking feet and smiles, looking older, as if I am the young one. He meets my eyes. "Are you with us?"

I don't look down. "Of course, I am."

God forgive me, of course, I am.

We take fifteen minutes looking at different ceremonies. It's almost six and the evening service is at seven o'clock. Religion is at convenient hours in this small town, late enough for people to finish dinner but early enough so that some can go on to parties. Even now choir members might be gathering. I ask them – are they ready? Oh, no. They don't mean to get married right away. They're not rushing. (No, of course, they aren't.) They are going to stay for the second service. They want to be married after that – when everyone has gone home, maybe nine o'clock.

How temperate and calmly considered of them.

Jess goes out to tell Maddy and Matt that everything is arranged. The two of them are going to organize a little dinner after the ceremony at a local Thai restaurant where Ben and Jaz, Anne and Thas will join them. I wonder about the shelf-life of a secret that Jaz is a party to or at a party for, but decide it's not my business.

Jess laughs. "We thought it would take longer to convince you."

I should have played more theologically hard to get?

Act 3. Scene 2. The sanctuary, two hours later.

I go through the next service in a bit of a daze. No one notices. Did I mention it is all about the choir? After the last handshake and season's greetings, I send the sexton away with good wishes to his family and a gift card to Home Depot. Do I know my staff or what? Leave everything, I tell him. It's five days till another service here.

Jess and Rashid and I move poinsettias around. Their favorite are red with white stripes. Maddy Rose and Matt return. Matt has been into the Christmas cheer and smells of it. I'm not thrilled, but they are presentable and I understand that Rashid doesn't want Ben to witness a wedding that will cause family problems, no matter how assimilated into the United States is his branch of the family. This way he can honestly say he was invited out to dinner on Christmas Eve and only then found out about the wedding.

And so they are married, Jess Carson and Rashid Mahmood, in a circle of relit candles and poinsettias, beside the manger with real hay, empty because a little girl took her doll away. Very simple vows. Their rings are rose gold and quite wide. Each has the other's name engraved inside and two blessings: *May the peace of Christ abide in your home* and in Arabic, *May Allah bless thee and may His blessings fall upon thee and He unite thee both in goodness.*

They kiss and the evening stops to watch them in their sweetness. Christmas Eve itself stands still.

They ask me out to the dinner because I won't take money. Well, in for a marriage license, in for a paradise pikpow I always say! And I have a wonderful time – I laugh with Jazmin and realize that Thas is gay. (How clueless am I anyway? I can set him up with a great support group for gay and lesbian teens in a neighboring town.) Matt gives an outrageous toast that gets applause from everyone in the restaurant. That should cancel the deepest secrecy part, you think? Then they leave, each to their own homes. No, *it is the east, and Juliet is the sun* for this young couple's wedding night. Jess wrinkles her nose and tells me her folks pulled out her stocking this year, something they had not hung since she was ten. Isn't that weird?

No, not weird. Isn't that sad and desperate and frightened? And, oh, if only there had been years of growing up with good communication to build on, how much easier this would all be.

For them and for me. I do feel sorry for them. Soon I will

probably be the villain. Tonight, honestly, it feels worth it.

I go home and get into my solitary bed, but there is so much young love in the atmosphere I can smell it. I pray for Jess and Rashid before I turn out the light. In the dark I pray for their families and for us all. I don't think to pray for Tim and Matt specifically. As it turns out, I should have done so.

Act 4. Scene 1. A full week later.

Remarkably a Thai restaurant full of people, Thas the adoring, Anne the symbiote, Jaz the chatty – none of the obvious suspects betray the young lovers' secret for a whole week. To be honest, Jazmin is visiting relatives in Vermont, but she has her tablet, her Smartphone, *and* she's bored, so I give her credit for prodigious willpower. The young lovers meet somehow and made plans. I am not a part of them. I send in the license, making sure the legalities of the marriage are in order. I assume that neither tells their family, but I still avoid every place I anticipate meeting the parents. I go grocery shopping on the way back from a meeting at the denominational headquarters in Pembroke so that even my purchase of tofu, bread and milk does not put me in their path.

And now it is New Year's Eve, a holiday of misrule if ever there was one. The older, theoretically wiser Matt lets the drinking take him where he should not go.

Tim and his cronies are eating fajitas and leering at girls in a restaurant. They had begun the Auld-Lang-Slide into inebriation earlier themselves. This Tex-Mex is the best place for take-out in town. Ben and Rashid pull up but stay in the car while Matt collects their order. He's sloshed with an empty stomach and it unleashes the Mercurial swagger never too far beneath the surface.

Tim starts it. "Hey, rag-head lover, Atta-boy, come in for some *American* food?"

"American food? You're eating fajitas, a-hole."

"Yeah, I'm an American all right. What you going to have – a little tahini, a little camel shit and dates?"

"You are just stupid."

"You're just sorry that your boy-toy Rashid was dumped by my cousin. She could find better ..." here there is a nasty gesture "... at the oasis.

"What do you mean? They're still together."

"Still together, are you kidding? They're history – like Osama bin Laden is history! Big history. She doesn't want any of that burka-shit, I can tell you that. Yeah she is heading just about as far from him as she can go! "

Matt mumbled, "On the way to her honeymoon."

"What did you say, you moron?"

"I said," and he enunciates very distinctly, or so I have been told, "I *said* that Jess and Rashid are not heading anywhere but to their honeymoon, jerk-off. Fooled you. Fooled all of you. Plague on your crappy bigoted houses!"

And he storms out. Tim is on his heels. Someone tries to give Matt his take-away but he brushes it aside. He slams the door behind him and it smacks the younger boy.

Just outside the door on the deck with a trash barrel and a cigarette tower is a bucket of sand to keep the stairs from becoming slippery and a steel shovel.

Tim snatches it with both hands and starts to run. For moments they are on stage, crossing the parking lot, lit up by the lights.

Tim catches him up and hits him hard with the shovel. Matt goes down like a stone. Ben leaps out of Rashid's idling car and runs over to look at Matt. Tim doesn't stop. He slams into that sweet little BMW, throws it into reverse and guns it straight backward into the old Volvo that Rashid drives around because his doting grandmother gave it to him. "Safest thing a boy like you can be in. Like a tank."

It is solid and safe and Rashid is in a seat belt. Tim isn't and the impact sends him through the windshield. The glass and the maple tree are unforgiving.

One minute maybe from Matt's slip of the lip to a dead boy

and a concussed one lying on the ground. Rashid is shaking as he crawls out of the passenger's side door and throws up in the bushes. Ben goes over and puts an arm around him. Twenty or thirty calls to 911 and the police arrive and the EMT's, but for Tim it is all too late.

They take Rashid and Ben to the station for their evidence but they are released – sitting in a parked car that is hit by a driver who has just battered someone with a shovel is not a chargeable offense ... except in a small town that needs to blame someone, like the immigrant survivor of an accident that's taken the life of a hometown boy.

Act 4. Scene 2.

Matt's father won't speak to Rashid at the hospital and his mother just whispers, "I wish my son had never got mixed up with you people." It's two days before he wakes up, and there may be neurological damage, the cautious hospitalist says. Tim Carson's service is in the town's largest funeral home. Jess attends, white and strained and hollow-eyed. She doesn't sit with her parents or Anne. Rashid does not come. He doesn't want to cause any more pain.

Because that is how he feels – he believes their love bred the whirlwind that blew out the spirit of one young man and perhaps changed another forever. And he, even without an angel's warning, is fleeing to Egypt. Without Jess. He has family there, an uncle with a coffee shop. The uncle makes arrangements, no questions asked. If all works out, perhaps one of his children will come to America and stay with Rashid's parents and the twins. Rashid will have a gap year. His college acceptances will trickle in and he will decide in a small town near Cairo what he is going to do. With his life. With the heart that he is planning on wrapping up and putting away forever.

Rashid ignores Jess' texts, her emails, her phone calls. She wants to come with him. She wants to talk to him face to face. She wants to explain to him in logic that cannot be denied why he's not to blame, why she's not to blame (why I'm not to blame).

That's how I get into it again. Again. The Epiphany plot. I'll be driving Rashid to the Manchester Airport on Epiphany, January 6. His parents know that he's going. They disapprove. They think leaving town is acting guilty and, although they were against his dating Jess, they are adamant that he had the right to do so.

They are not going to enable this running away behavior. Egyptians do not do that. Palestinians do not do that. Rashid looks at them. They know he thinks coming to the United States is a kind of running away. They ran *toward* a future for him and his five year old sisters.

That he is married – no, they don't know that. Nobody but some teenagers know that. And me. How exposed can I get? In for a friar, in for a liar.

"I'll help you see him one more time," I promise her. I have a plan. It can only work if he is so dazed with loss and remorse that he doesn't think very much.

"How can he leave me?"

It is there in her face – fear that he is going to a region that this autumn contains new terrorists who do unspeakable things. He will be unsafe. She won't be there to … well, whatever it is women want to do to protect the ones they love. She can't say this to him because it sounds like irrational fear of Muslims, and Jess could not bear Rashid believing that she was, indeed, her parents' child.

"The thing is, Jess, he isn't thinking of you right now except as part of something that went terribly, terribly wrong." I can see I am hurting her but it is the truth. She is going to need to live with this truth if he goes to Egypt. She is right. This isn't marriage. Marriage is where, if nothing else, you promise to *talk* about better and worse, sickness and health, but of course, there are people twice their age who can't do it.

And so I say to him, just as casually as I can. "Take the Volvo to the boarded up fruit stand this afternoon and park it there with your luggage. I'll meet you and drive you home." His parents are throwing a small dinner for him and I am invited by his mother as the outsider who functions to keep all the tempers in check. It is a familiar clergy role. "In the morning you bike out, throw the bike in the car and wait for me. I'll get dropped off by one of my regular clergy breakfast friends so I can take you to Manchester Airport, get your car home and zip over to the church on your bike. Your folks can pick it up once they cool down ... Rashid?"

"Yeah. thanks. I appreciate it." He doesn't blink. He doesn't think "why so labyrinthine?" He doesn't think much at all. I get away with it.

Because I know he is expecting it, I ask him, "Do you want to talk about it?"

"Nothing to talk about."

"Jess, I'll leave you in his car. He'll be on his bike and will need to get in to be warm. I'll give you twenty minutes to talk then I'll come back. I hope you can pull him out of it. Get him to start talking. He's locking it up inside. And Jess? Divorce or a future together – whatever happens, I'll help."

"Not divorce. Never, never divorce. I love him too much. He loves me."

"And he's suffering PTSD worse than anything he could have experienced in the Mideast. Or maybe not, but certainly it is much more personal. Two weeks ago he was ten years younger and he sees you still on that side. It's a self-dug chasm he can't cross."

"I can't live without him. I can't!"

"Yes Jess, you can. You will."

"Why? Why should I live?"

This is actually my territory.

"You will live to give him time. You will give him all the time he needs. He would give it to you."

"I would never want it."

"Everyone, at some time in their life needs time and space. You will let him go, if he needs to go and you will wait, if you know anything about love."

She looks at me for a long, long time.

"Jess?"

"Yes?" she asks.

"There was something about a baby?"

"I was wrong."

I wonder, but I just stay silent. She is thinking.

"I'll wait for him, of course I will. First I'll try to convince him not to go. Stay here. Get therapy."

"Good girl."

Act 4. Scene 3.

It was a plan. And it should have worked but Jess is both exhausted and so overwrought that she swallows two of her mother's valiums thinking that they'll make her calmer. No, it has nothing to do with my herbs. Just my stupid plan. Jess sits in that cold car on January 6, Three Kings Day, day of gifts and strange visitations from the east, and she wraps up in a car robe, goes under the seat mat for the key, and turns on the ignition. When Rashid arrives she is lying in the back seat deeply asleep, or maybe passed out. I don't know, and even if I anticipated she'd know how to find the key and would be crazy enough to turn on the car, surely she'd open a window. Honestly, that old Volvo is drafty enough at the best of times. Sleeping, she is sleeping.

But Rashid thinks she is dead. Carbon monoxide. You knew that was coming – you were waiting for it. *A pair of star-cross'd lovers* ... After he shakes her and cries and panics and dials 911 and then hangs up, he closes the car up tight and he stuffs his wool cap in the exhaust pipe, because he is going to die with her.

Does she wake up and see him and decide to stay and die? I don't know. This isn't some god damned play, but they are wrapped in each other's arms, when I get there.

Early.

I get there early. Early enough.

I go earlier than I promised. I decide (perhaps because it is Epiphany and some holy something sends me a star) not to give them even twenty minutes to talk alone. And so I get there in time. Less than two minutes after he closes up the car and takes her in his arms. When I see that car running with a blocked exhaust, I run like someone is ripping out my heart. I jerk the door open, cough and drag them out, heads bumping. I slap them and give them mouth to mouth, back and forth, crazy and ineffective, and shake them and feel the thin, thin thread of breath. I drag them, both sputtering and Jess throwing up, into my car and head for the hospital where oxygen is administered and the troopers who picked up the 911 arrive with a lot of paper work.

Act 5.

Jess and Rashid do not die. The jury is still out whether they will thank me for the friar-deflected suicide. Their parents are wild with fear. The high school population is titillated and curious. Their romantic tragedy has become a survivor story. They are going to have a messy life. Isn't that just the way that any contemporary teenager story goes if there are no vampires?

Besides the survival? In these ways their story is different from *Romeo and Juliet*. Jess and Rashid's parents are not going to erect gold statues to their love or make peace, although Bahiti Mahmood, Rashid's mother, and Jeff Carson are acting more conciliatory than their children have any reason to hope. Ahmed and Joan are still not even talking to God, much less their spouses or children. Patrick is very confused. Ben and Jazmin broke up. It's collateral damage, but they weren't that serious. Everyone knows Jess and Rashid are married because Madison Rose sent a beautiful photograph of the Christmas Eve wedding with the poinsettias, the straw-filled manger and my dopey smiling face into the local paper. To date, I am still employed.

I'm the friar. I am the one who is here to say it doesn't have to end that way. In tragedy. When it is a tragedy, the parents are supposed to win and repent. They didn't win and they didn't repent. I'm the friar and I am here to say that the ones who love a forbidden love, even the silly and foolish ones in love with love itself, don't have to die. I'm the friar and you really know more about me than you ever wanted to know. *Romeo and Juliet* is about the kids, isn't it? No, it's about somebody, anybody, standing up and telling the adults they have to stop misbehaving. Stick that in your Epiphany and light it. While you're at it, light the world.

Oh, yes, unlike the Bard's Friar Lawrence, I'm not going to run away.

I never could put a love story down.

THE SHAKESPEARE READER

At Christmas I no more desire a rose,
Than wish a snow in May's new-fangled mirth;
But like of each thing that in season grows.
Love's Labours Lost

The Shakespeare Reader settled into the maroon chair and looked with favor at his Christmas cactus simply bursting with buds. It was the season for the Christmas cactus, not the rose. It was an old, practically antique Christmas cactus. Sometimes it was off by a few weeks, but the old are allowed to be a bit off!

There was a crash in the hall. "Can't catch me!" ... a high-pitched squeal.

"Wait for me!" the sound of a tussle.

He was out of his chair. Something was happening. Call 911 or check it out first? He chose both – pulled out the cell phone and pulled open the door. More crashing about and running ... and squealing and giggling.

The female voice. "You're not my boyfriend. Leave me alone." She was short, pert and blond. Tight jeans, cute shoes and not really in distress.

He was pie-eyed, lovelorn and foolish with it. Basketball tall with brown hair, retro-frame glasses and stylishly clashing clothes. Nerdy but not completely clueless. Some girl's idea of a dream come true. Not this girl's. He was panting a little (maybe he didn't play basketball) and not dangerous at all. "Look, I didn't mean anything. I mean, I'm sorry. I just wanted ..."

Hands on her hips. "You wanted what, exactly? A hook-up. Nope, nope, nope." Wagging the finger all naughty-boy and come-hither at the same moment. "I'm taken. We are going to Disney next weekend. Can't go to the Magic Kingdom with him and mess around with you."

"But just give me a chance. I'll take you somewhere. I promise."

"No way! Besides don't you haaaave (she drew it out) a 'girlfriend?' Seems like I heard that somewhere. Oh, yeah, she told me. Surprise! Your 'girlfriend' told me she was your girlfriend!" She kissed her fingers and blew a sweet and fairy-dusted kiss at him and he leaped up to catch it in pantomime.

The Hermia was gone, out the front door with the Demetrius helplessly following. The Shakespeare Reader looked after them and then glanced up. Yes, inevitable. The Helena was there in the stairwell, a floor and a half up. She was tall and model thin, starvation thin (the thin of a girl who thinks another pound is going to make all the difference) with long brown hair she had just perfectly straightened. Her nose was straight. Her eyebrows were straight. There were tears on her face. He turned and went back into his apartment and shut the door quietly, very quietly, and found his chair again.

He was the Shakespeare Reader. He had been reading Shakespeare for a long time. He drew out a facsimile folio that he had purchased on his vacation last month. *Richard II*. Now that was a bad death. He looked over at his coffee table. Everything was here for a lovely, quiet evening, An old man's evening. He chuckled just a little at himself. There was tea, hot in the pot and Mrs. Garrity's homemade ginger cookies. A bottle of wine and a glass were arranged for later. In the kitchen there was bread in the bread maker and soup in the slow cooker. The house smelled delicious.

Mrs. Garrity was a Mistress Quickly, comfortable and loving, and she cared about him, (in spite of perennially getting his phone messages and visits -- even visits from the police -- completely confused). She would proudly quote -- *He hath eaten me out of house and home, he hath put all my substance into that fat belly of his.* And then she would laugh, her hands on her hips staring at his slight figure – so opposite to Falstaff. But it was one of the two Shakespeare lines she'd learned for everyday use with her unusual employer who had, as she affectionately said, his "hobby."

Her coat already on, she asked, "Just those college kids chasing around?"

"Yes, though at their age, one's laughter often means another's tears."

"Most any age that could be true."

Before she left, Mrs. Garrity played a word on the open Scrabble game that always sat on a fold-out table by the door. She played "Arden," as in "the forest of Arden," from the "a" in "Sylvia." All words in his Scrabble game must be Shakespeare, but he kept a little notebook with a list of possibilities so visitors could play as they pulled off coats and boots. There were always ten letters exposed, no racks. A game took weeks. He played "Tybalt" off the "y" in Sylvia and poured out the cup of tea. Probably he would curse himself later for boxing himself in too tightly. No winners or losers. The play's the thing ...

And off she went, malaprop and dear with her other hard-learned Mistress Quickly line tossed over her shoulder, *"Well, fare thee well."*

And he, as always, "Fare thee well, Mrs. Garrity.

He was the Shakespeare Reader. He called himself Ben. It was for Benedict, of course. His Beatrice had made him a Benedict and how he missed her – his beautiful feisty wife, the challenge and the love of his life. Like the original characters *in Much Ado About Nothing,* when friends brought them together, there was endless sparring. It was the sparring that they both adored. Jibe, riposte, clever remark, pause for planning the perfect retort.

Beatrice to him. *"I had rather hear my dog bark at a crow, than a man swear he loves me."* Well, actually she used a more contemporary version of the same thing.

And he would reply. *"I wish my horse had the speed of your tongue."* Of course, sometimes he said "Jetta." It was delicious.

When they reached their forties those friends decided they needed to settle down and play the part of a respectable couple. *When I said I would die a bachelor, I did not think I should live till I were married.* And that too was play-perfect -- each fooled into thinking the other was a shy but doting lover.

Ben to Beatrice, *"Come, I will have thee, but by this light, I take thee for pity."*

And she to him, *"I yield upon great persuasion, and partly to save your life, for I was told you were in a consumption."*

Or – "needed a triple bypass." or "could cash in your chips."

And he to her, *"Peace. I will stop your mouth."*

And he did so with a kiss. In the end, with many, many kisses.

Now she was gone. The cancer ate through her like frost through a rose of May, and she had left him here. He hardly remembered what his name had been before he knew he was a Benedict.

Ben ate a ginger cookie and swallowed some tea without tasting much.

The apartment walls and ceilings were thin. He could hear his upstairs neighbors, a Prospero and Ariel moving around, getting ready for their supper. They were an uncle and grand-niece and there was love between them, but a strange love – a bound love, a slave love, the girl needing to be free, and the older man preventing it. She needed to be of the air, to travel, to write her poetry and starve if that's what that meant.

Prospero was a failed professor of something - economics or sociology – something that makes a man wise about large scale human behavior and foolish in the little politics of families, and that most dysfunctional family of them all – a university. His exile was a trumped-up case hard to prove, but proof is not essential in a world where even one hint of misconduct with a young female student is two hints too many. His closest friend and protégé Cal had betrayed him and now had his position. So Ben's upstairs neighbor, whose real name was not actually Prospero, but close enough at Prof O__ something, sat among his books, plotting his revenge. In paralleling to *Tempest,* Cal was in the wrong role for his name and there was no Miranda, but, like his mentor, Ben did not follow the source material slavishly.

Prof O's grand-niece, whose divorced parents were too over-busy in their own lives to spend time with an adult daughter, ran Prospero's errands and edited his forthcoming book for room and board and a stipend, but she did it with limp wings. Well, living with a person who is always thinking about revenge doesn't really lift the spirits. This Ariel was also a Starbucks barista and she left for that job with a bounce in her step and came back with all the campus news. The young woman enjoyed the Trinculo-ing of the passing crowd, and told the daily tale with flourish, but she, unlike the Hermias and Lysanders of the upper floors longed not for love, not for social media, but for autonomy. *"Where the bee sucks, there suck I In the cow-slip's bell I lie ..."*

Ariel. She was an Ariel. Ariel would come downstairs to visit Ben, fit in a Scrabble word, and tell him of passing Stephanos and Ferdinands and how the poison gnawing away at her uncle's soul was eating her life as well. Ben was a great listener – perhaps that really was his gift. Everyone visited Ben, and talked. And Ariel's gift in exchange for his listening? Fond as he was of Mrs. Garrity's ubiquitous tea, Starbucks lattes were a wondrous wickedness. Forget alcohol. Ben became a veritable tosspot of coffee and Ariel his Tempest temptress.

"You need a dog," Ariel had said the previous July. "You don't get out in the fresh air enough. You are going to turn *into* a book. Or, excuse me, a frickin' *folio*. Not a good thing." She barely hid her concern that after Beatrice's death he didn't want to do much of anything. Bossy as the daughter he didn't have, she dragged him to the shelter and made him choose. Cressida met his eyes through the cage and wagged helicopter. Her owner had died and she was ten – not prime time for adoption. Widower and wid-dog had suited each other. The fresh air therapy worked better in July, even September. "Shall I compare December 22 to a summer's day?" he muttered.

He bribed the dog with leftover bread. Cress could smell Mrs. Garrity's stew.

"No licking the pot! Want to go out?"

Slow but wagging, with her black beard and baritona bark, she was adequate protection. Ben bundled up for the still snowless cold. "Lonely old man walks plump dog past Christmas lights," he imagined the Cambridge photojournalist caption. Wind hit them at the top of the front steps. Cress, even with her thick coat and bulk, turned sideways. Ben pulled hat down and collar up and, ducking, saw into what the landlord called the garden apartment ... and everyone else called basement flat. There sat Ian, spotlighted by a single bulb, nursing a glass of whiskey. Scotch, Ben thought. The Iago was probably a Scotch drinker. Home alone. The Desdemona would be at work waiting tables at the restaurant; the Othello would be at the center of some social fling.

Ian Hunter, a rather ordinary thirty-two year old vet with dishwater blond hair, a broken sideways nose, and the feel of an Iago, looked up and raised his glass to toast. Ben lifted a hand in response and cursed himself for always being suspicious. Then he shivered. Ian couldn't see a dark man in a navy coat with a black dog. He sat in the only pool of light. They stood outside in the dark. So who or what was Ian toasting? And there was a revolver on the table. Chilled by more than the season, Ben dragged Cress down Brattle Street to the Cambridge Common with its lit holiday trees. A thinking walk – not quite Danish battlements, but he was reading Shakespeare.

Yes, it made him suspicious.

Ben loved all things Shakespeare. When he had several glasses of wine, he would see them -- pucks tumbling, fairies cavorting, brooding monarchs lurking and plotting and calling for horses, wondrous lovers – especially girls dressed as boys who confused boys. So would a lonely evening pass between the page and the dream.

But just passing the time with a book on his lap was not *how* he was a Shakespeare Reader. He was *the* Shakespeare Reader. He read the Shakespeare that was hidden in people. He saw the Portia in the Prospect Street lawyer, the Messina watch in the officers called to break up the Central Square party, the Polonius in his own slimy brother-in-law who was always insinuating himself into Ben's affairs. Oh, for a curtain, a dagger, and castle shadows!

Through some kind of psychic twist Benedict was able to read the Shakespeare plot mirrored by a person or a situation. Those plots worked on stage so well because they were all too real in human life. Not a mind-reader, an empath, or a future see-er, and not even a deductive genius like Sherlock Holmes. Just a retired man with a paranormal bent for the Bard who knew everyone for blocks around. Mostly it was fun – a game. Sometimes, like tonight, it was uncomfortable. On occasion though, even the police had been known to consult.

It began with the Lear murder. Simple even for a non-Shakespeare reader, but plain as day to Ben. A father with three grown daughters lived in the neighborhood in a beautiful old Victorian. The city grew grubby around its walls for many years, but real estate value returned and then it soared. This father disowned his youngest daughter, saying she did not love him. She (whom Ben mentally called Cordelia but whose real name was Carol) was honest about his memory loss and dared to recommend a neurologist. She mentioned Aricept and Namenda and suggested, ever so gently, that he move somewhere with twenty-four seven assistance. She never said nursing home. With his resources he would have a wide spectrum of living arrangements to choose from. But there would be help, care, people glad to keep him safe. Of course, it would tap his resources – Cordelia didn't care – she wasn't waiting for his bundles of money.

Wrong thing to say.

How dare she not be waiting for his benevolence! Love him and not his money? Did she think he was a fool? *How sharper than a serpent's tooth it is to have a thankless child!* He packed her off to live with a former college roommate. "Out, out, out!" The other sisters were smooth of tongue, flattering. The middle daughter (Ben called her Regan) once said at a holiday gathering, clearly within her father's hearing, "Age just passed my Dad by." It made Ben, born the same year as Lear and well-aware of his own aggravating aphasia lapses, want to gag.

So the old man stayed with two daughters in his family home, though they were rarely there, never cooked a meal, didn't clean up or do laundry. Lear had a friend, an old army buddy, who hung around for the poker, the gab, and watching ESPN, but the two daughters found this Fool overly sharp-eyed. Neil made a few too many comments about how much they were not around and then he wasn't welcome anymore.

Lear was murdered during a break-in. Of course, it was the only "target house" on the block. Regan and Goneril wept buckets of alligator tears to match their pocketbook-motives, then quickly planned a memorial service and mercy meal. Ben made a condolence call. A not-very-mournful daughter sat opposite him in the largest room. It was the other one, but even Ben couldn't call a contemporary woman 'Goneril.' He watched her assess whether he would require an invitation to the mercy meal.

Mentally he called her, 'Cheap Bitch.'

"Terrible. Think of it …" he said, making small talk, "imagine smothering an old man with a pillow and only taking an ancient desktop computer and costume jewelry, while leaving the tablet and high-end sound equipment?" Break-in? Really? Get a clue. Ben knew what had to be the truth. This plot was as modern as it was Elizabethan. Children waiting for an old man to die, afraid he'll run through too much money before considerately bowing off the stage.

Clues, however, were not Ben's expertise. He applied to a lieutenant Dogberry whose course of investigation was following up recently released burglars. Ben was fairly sure pros didn't bother to kill old guys with dementia. And crackheads would tear everything apart looking for stuff to hock. Strange, how neat the house was.

Ben wondered when it would go on the market.

Dogberry and her fellows got tired of Ben camping out at headquarters, drinking cop coffee, offering his Penguin *King Lear* to anyone who'd read it. Still, pushed by his persistence and the scarcity of other leads, she started hunting for clues. And she found them too, not that she publicly credited Ben, the rankest of amateur sleuths, but the assistant district attorney was called in.

Ben's Bard-alert to what might come next saved Cordelia's life from her increasingly reckless sisters. They were crazy enough to kill her. He knew it. If he could not get anyone to believe him, he would knock her door down, even though he was an old guy. Thank God it was unlocked because he probably couldn't have gotten the job done. So, yes, he did save her. Along with EMTs and a stomach pump. He quoted his precious script then. Inappropriately, but never mind. *"This feather stirs; she lives! If it be so, it is a chance which does redeem all sorrows that ever I have felt."*

The police respected Ben's strange talent ever since that time. It was a unique talent, paranormal, maybe, forensic occasionally. Some retired people become attached to cats or gardens or volunteer jobs. The Shakespeare Reader read plots all around him and fumbled a little stage-management. Like now, when he guessed there was an Iago toasting a plan in the basement flat.

Back at his apartment, Cress curled into a very tight ball to warm up and Ben emailed Dogberry that he was going to drop by tomorrow and lay it all out – what he suspected, what he had seen, what he feared, the Shakespeare he *read*.

Julius Caesar in the play of the same name advises sound sleeping. Having made a start, Ben took the emperor's advice. Of course, how did that work out for Julius?

"Moved in eight months ago or so. Gay couple, got engaged at Thanksgiving. Thello is probably post-the-most of his PTSD. He's confident, and stable in public but careful of his own emotions, particularly his temper. Ian's an army friend. Dishonorable discharge."

Her hands hovered over the computer, so he quickly went on. "No criminal action. Something happened in Kabul. Hushed up. So he came to visit and just happened to stay."

"Just stay?"

"Thello's the kind of person willing to take a friend's side for the sake of days they rode a hummer together and wondered what rock would explode. *One that loved not wisely but too well.*"

"Ben – spit it out." The homicide detective did not have time for this.

"One's a softie, one's a snake."

"OK. Poor judgment on softie's part. You're here, why?"

"Des. Thello's love. A sweet man with a laugh like dawn birds. I think Des is in danger. *O, beware of jealousy, the green-eyed monster that mocks the meat it feeds on.*"

"Three gay guys in one apartment. Jealousy. Tell me something newsworthy."

Oh, Ian isn't gay. And it isn't envy of the love. It's Thello's success. The restaurant, the celebrity, the TV stuff."

Dogberry sat up abruptly. "That Thello! The Thello of Thello's? You live in the same building as Thello? We have an anniversary coming up. I don't suppose you could get reservations. Tony watches him on "Meat-Chefs -- The Bloody Darlings.""

Ben knew that her husband, Tony, the math teacher, did the cooking. Homicide could be stressful, but high school was worse. Tony really needed to de-stress after a day's work. The detective continued in a rather dreamy tone. "We've had broiled chops with pomegranate tears and sliced hangar steak with jalapeno commas. To die for, if you know what I mean."

Ben smiled, "In your business, my dear, it means a lot! Thello is the sweetheart of the charity world – always donating food or his entertaining performance preparing it. Raised in a ghetto. GED, then military, six months in a culinary institute, caught the eye of a very rich African American entrepreneur who staked him to his own restaurant. And he's been paying it forward ever since – he's a success *and* a walking inspirational story. He's even given a university commencement address. Consider that.

"Ian's a college grad with nothing to show for it. No wonder envy eats him alive. Thello's just clueless. He gave Ian a job waiting tables at the restaurant and thought he would be grateful. After all, Des loves it there, brightens customers with that megawatt smile and makes buckets of tips that sustain him between little theatre jobs. I can't imagine the brooding ex-vet as a tip-magnet. Then Thello offered Ian the spare bedroom."

Dogberry winced. "Stupid. I see that."

"So I'm taking the trash to the curb one evening and Ian actually said, in a voice like he was taunting someone not present and drunk for sure. 'Have you heard – I'm a waiter? Oh, yes, I am, old man. I am a *waiter* now.' And I thought ... he's waiting all right. There's a smothering hovering."

"What?" She was confused.

"*Othello*. The play? The motive's there. Method doesn't matter as much. I can't read what it will be. Death by smothering. But also maybe a shot in the dark, or a knife. Ian will plan it, but Thello will go down for it. Ian will stack up the kindling of jealousy in his friend's mind and light it with the PTSD that's always just shy of a flash. Later he will be so apologetic. He'll say he was mistaken – he thought he was telling Thello the truth about an affair of Des with ... well, Cassio-whoever, as long as some small taste of racism sickens the black chef's stomach till it burns his heart."

Ben wrapped up this "read" for his Dogberry. She pushed purple-tinted auburn hair off her forehead and asked bluntly, "What exactly am I supposed to do with that?"

"Prevent a crime before Christmas, of course."

"Ben, I'm a homicide detective. That means I work with the *un-prevented* crimes. You're a Do-gooder – an unusual, unique Do-gooder, I grant you, but it's more your line to ..."

"Tell Thello I think his old army buddy is going to convince him to strangle or smother or stab or shoot his lover because of a suspicion of unfaithfulness? And, by the way, I think this is because of the similarity between their situation and the plot of a play by William Shakespeare written round about 1602. What would you lay on my chances?"

"I'm listening to you."

"Touché."

"Honestly, he won't believe you, but if it started to happen, he would remember that you had predicted something like this and he'd be cautious."

"Cautious PTSD? Like that's going to happen."

"Ben, I like you and I trust that you are not crazy. I'm not sure why I do, but I do. You saved Carol Laverly's life when her sisters set her up for a remorse suicide for mercy killing her demented father on the off chance that we didn't buy the break-in theory. Their second line of defense conveniently eliminated a third heir. You got us there, and, then, because you were ahead of us and not too picky about a little B and E yourself, you saved her."

"Unlocked, remember, unlocked."

She reached over and adjusted the frame of four-year old Aggie's photograph on her desk. She had set the digital frame slow – every thirty seconds a new picture. Then she reached over and adjusted the dog, Smut, a cross between a Yorkie and a dachshund. Satisfied, she looked up. "Yes, and you kept at me ... us ... until we went after the old man's death as a possible premeditated homicide instead of the by-product of a burglary. You were right then, too. But somebody had already died! For God's sake, I've got no business at all in this inter-personal situation. I can't do anything."

"Could you run a background check? If a heavy-duty police check flags Ian, Thello might listen to me."

She stared into the middle distance and tapped her fingernails on her desk. She stopped. It was a new manicure, Christmas red, and she didn't want them ruined before Tony even saw them. Manicures were extravagant. "Use of departmental resources, Ben. It's money. Money I could not justify upstairs. Bring me a body. I do things with bodies."

"That's just tedious – a very tedious brief, indeed. You should prevent the proliferation of bodies. Surely having unnecessary corpses could be considered an even more costly way of wasting the department's resources."

"That's not how city government works."

"Tedious bureaucracy! I do have another idea though, and with this you can help me, my dear Dogsy."

She winced at the nickname then noticed how many emails had gone unattended since he had been sitting there. Time to move the local color on. "Hope your idea involves finishing that cup of *free* departmental coffee and heading back to your apartment to keep an eye on potential miscreant rogues of Bardic bent and that big sweet terrier."

"This cup is so indescribably awful that, free or not, I'll leave it unfinished. My idea involves the purchase of a rather large Douglas fir, dragging it up to my apartment, acquiring the fixings for a perfect eggnog, and a cider to spice and mull for the less alcohol-inclined. Nobody will drink sack, will they?"

"Nobody in my acquaintance drinks anything called sack, though some drink just about anything out of a sack. Mostly we make do with this brew."

"I shudder for your internal organs, but, yes, I promise coffee, Starbucks coffee. My dear Dogberry, methinks I may invite you and the inestimable Tony and sweet Aggie to a tree trimming at my apartment on Friday night. I draw the line at Smut. He can't be trusted with trees, and he most certainly cannot be trusted with Cress."

"Smut comes up to her knees and is no longer of any concern to any bitch, however historically wayward. But he prefers home to a crowd. Is there an agenda for this tree-trimming evening?"

"The agenda for a tree-trimming would seem obvious. We will decorate my humble abode through group effort and pleasant community. Needing additional enticement, I will be serving the most sought after appetizers in all of Boston made by my ground floor neighbor and purchased by me two months ago at a charity auction. They will be delicious beyond compare and Thello himself will be present ..."

"As will Des and your Iago. This is entrapment. Delectable and almost irresistible entrapment, but nevertheless. ..."

"There will also be served a lovely selection of my neighbors and friends. You are already acquainted with Carol and she will be delighted to see you again. You don't stand out as law enforcement and I think Tony is adamant that you do not mix social and sociopath. Tell me you'll come."

She paused for a long moment but they both knew that she was just making him work for it. "I'll come. Tony and I, too, will be delighted to see Carol. We'll get a babysitter for Aggie. I actually have a rather vivid memory of your eggnog from last New Years Eve!"

"Ah my dear Dogsy ...*you are a wise fellow, and, which is more, an officer, and, which is more, a householder, and, which is more, as pretty a piece of flesh as any is in Messina, and one that knows the law...*"

"Ben!"

"I'm sorry. I meant I'm so glad you're coming. What?"

"Would it trouble you too much to think of me as, say as less Dogberry and more ... Horatio?"

"Horatio?"

"Yeah. It fits, it alliterates (is that a word?) with my real name and it is a lot more flattering. Honestly, I have made some wrong calls in my career but I have never begged to be called an 'ass.' And I read an article online that said Horatio was the first theatrical detective – you know, not *CSI Miami* Horatio Caine -- *Hamlet* ..."

Ben nodded.

She went on, " ...and *Hamlet* is the first real murder mystery. Horatio's always on stage. Like me. Has to deal with ramblings of a crazy protagonist."

Ben laughed and she met his eyes and laughed, too. He bowed slightly as he vacated her visitor's chair. "Anything you wish – where there's a will, there's a skull."

It was, indeed, a big and beautiful tree, fit for a Denmark forest or a Dickens novel. He put lights carefully on it for hours – small ones and the bubbling kind that Beatrice loved so much. He blinked often to clear his eyes and the bubbles were even prettier. A soft breeze, like a gentle hand, dried one errant tear on his cheek. He twitched branches to get them just so. Boxes of ornaments were open for the guests to hang, and boxes of felt, sequins and glitter for those who liked DIY. One of the building's drippy Helenas was quite crafty. The lover crowd would be out in force so he hung mistletoe in dimly lit spots -- they could circle around and entertain themselves for an entire midwinter's eve.

Mrs. Garrity, as Mistress Quickly, had the sweet end of the holiday fare -- cookies and gingerbread characters and a fruitcake that looked pretty but would probably be avoided. It was trendy to dislike fruitcake without trying it. And that, in his not-so-humble opinion, was a passable definition of the word "trendy." Mrs. Garrity was very pleased with her contribution and would be long gone before a whiff of competition from the celebrity chef could be nosed out. And she had brewed a lovely large carafe of coffee. She pointed out that people who came to a late afternoon affair did not necessarily want to be carried out insensible or suffer from the digestive vagaries of hot cider. She would also be gone before Ariel arrived with more elaborate caffeination. La Quickly/Garrity didn't hold with tarting up good coffee.

Ben imagined that Horatia, as he was determined now to dub his really very shrewd detective, would take the carafe of honest joe option. She didn't go anywhere without her shoulder holster, and armed guests were best as sober guests.

As it was, the elderly housekeeper was barely out the door when Ariel arrived as if on the wind, with an armful of holly, bright with red berries, and a basket of biscotti as well as delightful holiday choices in coffee with syrups and sprinkles and whipped cream.

"Ben, I'm early. Is it OK?"

"Of course, my dear," and he was quick enough to catch her kiss on his cheek – such pretty chances were well worth his keeping nimble heels. "Your smile turns on the lights." He hit the switch and the tree glowed. The aptness of the timing made her laugh with pleasure and he realized he had not heard her laughing often these days.

"Your great-uncle is coming?"

"He wouldn't miss it, although he expects me to prod. I wanted to deliver this for you and set up the coffee bar ..." She caught sight of the pedestrian carafe and pointedly ignored it. "... before beginning the persuasion pas de deux. It goes like this ... yes, he is invited ... no, he is not a pariah and, yes, he must actually wear his corduroy jacket so that he looks like a professor in a stage sketch."

An unspoken question passed between them.

"Surely we won't be treated to Cal's company this evening. You didn't invite him?"

"Not particularly, but everyone's invited who knows someone else who's invited – it was pretty broad. All's well that ends well!" He shrugged.

"What you mean is that it's possible he'll just be passing in time to meet Thello and perhaps say something inexcusable. Actually, in my uncle's opinion, he doesn't have to say anything at all to be rendered inexcusable." She wrinkled her nose. Her hands were flying fast as fast – the coffee service, the holly in a large bowl on the dining table with a few lovely silver balls interspersed. The biscotti she put upright in little gold baskets with red napkins next to the coffee. "I'll be back to freshen this. What else can I do?"

"Nothing, everything is ready. Oh, what do you suggest for music?"

She paused, tipped her head to one side. "Classical but light when people gather – Nutcracker." When she saw him frown, "You don't want to challenge people while they set their emotional space in a room. Familiar tunes make them feel at home. Then, when things get going, a seasonal playlist – carols, secular traditional – you know, Silver Bells, Drummer Boy, BNL – old stuff. You know how to do this. You taught me!"

They looked at each other. "Bea taught you." But it was just a whisper to himself.

She left, a flash of brightness to jolly up old Prospero and convince him to come downstairs when it was perfectly obvious to both of them that he had been thinking about nothing else since he received a personal invitation. Invitations are rare for exiles.

The first guest to arrive was Carol Laverly – Ben's Cordelia. She was a comfortably round-figured woman of thirty-three who worked in a bookstore and loved all things book. Still it was too sensitive, in spite of that. He never called her Cordelia or mentioned that he "read" her as a character in *King Lear*. Some people knew he was the Shakespeare Reader; most thought he was some sort of Elizabethan history hobbyist. Ariel's name was Annie Oliver so the Ariel nickname didn't surprise folks. Ben always called her grandfather Prof O and Prof O liked to be reminded of the title very much.

Obviously Lieutenant Salvatore knew she was Shake-nicknamed and had made the decision to change her sobriquet. Ben had long ago discovered that she was not, in any respect, an "ass." He did know for a fact that Dog ... Horatia had not read a single

Shakespeare play when he first met her. After an Associate's degree in Criminal Justice from Bunker Hill Community College, she'd gone to the Police Academy and worked her way through the ranks. Bill Murray and Nathan Fillion playing the role of Dogberry in the movies lent it a mild cachet, but she was too street-wise not to recognize disrespect.

When he mentioned *Lear* she read it. Just like that. A clue is a clue. The Lieutenant didn't care if a clue was literary, culinary, veterinary or apothecary – it was homework to her. She had seen the similarity to the case in front of her and had been willing to follow Ben on it with raised eyebrows but with serious intent.

Since that time she had read more – including going back to *Much Ado about Nothing*. She asked him once if Ben was his "real name." He had looked at her silently. She had never known Bea and therefore didn't completely understand. A detective for a long time, she did know her interview technique. She revised the question. Was Ben his "original" name?

No.

She obviously went on a Bardic hunt for another character to fit their relationship and found Horatio – Horatio, yes, almost always on the stage, always the confidante and, a "plus" for her partner and child, given the final crime scene in Hamlet – a survivor.

Carol / Cordelia didn't have much personal life during the drama of living with her father or the drama of being kicked out of her father's house, or, in fact, the drama of almost being murdered. She wasn't married. She'd confided to Ben that, in a flutter of I'm-still-alive, she had joined Match.com and e-Harmony simultaneously and was having a wonderful time just dating anyone. Tonight, a tall sharp woman trailed her wearing a kanga. Kenya? Zambia? Malawi? Ben wondered. Further south? The jina was *Sitalipiza Na Wala Sitasahau.*

"Are we first? I'd like to introduce you to Esther Huso." Esther Huso was Titania. Pure Titania. Regal and deadly, but with the potential to be fond and foolish. Perhaps not a bad date choice for a woman with a history of overdoing responsibility. Time to play in the forest.

"So pleased to meet you. Carol's a dear friend of mine, and for her sake you're most welcome. We have cider, coffee, and eggnog with – if I do say so myself – a fine mingling of spirits."

Esther's voice was low and husky, with the slightest of accents, "I would love some of your wicked eggnog."

Ben hoped no Bottoms would arrive unexpectedly so the fairy doting could be reserved for Carol. She deserved some dote. On the other hand, ass heads could be considered a staple of holiday parties. He dipped the two women each a cup of foolish just as the doorbell rang and a little flurry of Lysander, Demetrius, Helena, Hermia and *As You Like It* forest lords came in. He remembered real names (mostly Matthew and Megan) long enough to make introductions. The aging of her parent had aged Carol, he thought. Contemporary, she was also a world apart from these university students and "on the way to the cubicle, gym, club" kids.

Des and Ian Hunter arrived at the same time as this crowd but appeared to have come separately from each other. Both were blond, but there the similarity ended. Des was short and slight, a dancer who moved with ease across the floor and stood at rest in first position. He was comfortable in his skin and comfortable with any company. Perfect as a waiter, perfect for a party.

And Nutcracker was the perfect score. Thank you, Ariel. Everyone was practically dancing as they sipped and dipped biscotti into hot or creamy beverages. Ben feared for Mrs. Garrity's pride until he noticed Titania licking a frosted gingerbread man. She bit the head off fiercely. A hopeful Orlando en route to introduce himself made a knee-jerk detour.

In contrast, Ian seemed uncomfortable in every way and certainly had already indulged in what, in his case, was not holiday "cheer." He moved from the door to the drinks in a direct line that bisected several ongoing conversations. No apologies. A little wake of awkward followed him. Arriving at the table, he turned to

Cordelia, and with a clown-like stage leer asked a little too loudly, "eggnog or cider – how do you take your roofies?"

In the stunned silence, she opened her mouth but a response simply wouldn't come. It was only a moment. She smiled, obviously deciding he could not possibly know she nearly died of a poisoned drink. She purposely misunderstood him. "I recommend the eggnog, if you are hoping to get goofy."

He took the glass without any thanks, downed it and held it out again. She dipped it full and was grateful to feel Titania's tall presence rising behind her, hooded as a cobra. The African woman asked, "Is this the music when the good toys fight the rat king?"

Next arrived Prof O in his corduroy with elbow patches, thistle row of eyebrows, and big magic hands. Ariel was on his arm, a twinkle of delight in a little black sequined dress with a bright red scarf. She air kissed everyone while her great uncle glowered and drank cider in the corner, as if his deep thoughts couldn't be bothered. Curiously enough, his corner had the best view of the door. Even he was a star-seeker.

Emilia, whose real name was, in fact, Emily Barnum, was in Ben's book group and worked at the branch library. A comfortable woman of a certain age, she angled to be noticed, noticed by Ben. Ben had not found a way to share with her that he preferred a woman of wit rather than a woman of pillow. He was sure there were men out there who wanted plush and easy companionship, but, alas, he could never imagine saying to this uncomplicated woman, *"For which of my bad parts didst thou first fall in love with me?"*

No, Emily Barnum might like to be married again and look as widow to find a nice widower, but she could as successfully set her cap at the stormy professor. Now there was an idea. Prof O was divorced – three or four, maybe half a dozen times. Emilia's first husband had been a jerk Iago-style. He would talk then trouble followed; somehow he was never around for the aftermath.

The thing about being a Shakespeare Reader was that he absolutely did *not* believe the plots had to play themselves out.

Cordelia lived. Emilia might tame the professor ... or someone. Presidents need not be assassinated, young women need not lose their hands and, he believed in his deepest being, that someday not even the deepest bigotry could keep star-crossed lovers apart.

Could villainy keep a lover and a star apart? Ben watched the crowd, pleased with sweet new acquaintances and the small exclamations of pleasant recognition between old friends. Des was partaking in both introductions and reconnections with the natural grace of a social animal, moving from group to group while waiting for Thello. Ian hovered like Poe's raven over the Scrabble board and the nevermore in his posture kept potentially friendly partygoers at a safe distance. His eyes followed Des and his iPhone recorded Des' progress – any smile, any laugh, certainly every small touch. Click and wait and click and wait. Like a deathwatch beetle in the wall.

Telltale Heart? Ben shook himself – he was the Shakespeare Reader, not the Poe Reader. Let someone else scan the world through those stories – he let *Twelfth Night* remind him of his hostly duties. *Do you think because you are virtuous, that there shall be no more cakes and ale?* He would worry later.

Emily, the book group scheduler, was also useful in practical ways. She immediately organized the younger crowd to decorate the tree. To Ben's surprise, almost everyone had brought him an ornament as a gift. Bardic expertise didn't translate to contemporary social niceties, and he had not realized this was the appropriately tasteful thing for a tree-trimming party. He opened and admired lovely ornaments, some elegant (the angel from Esther/Titania really was a fairy queen) and some attempting to be humorous (a red neck Santa, a tipsy Rudolph). Some were even handmade. Ariel embroidered silver stars on a deep blue velvet sky and pinned it with pearl pins on a ball. Emilia shellacked a gingerbread boy. Des offered him a tiny glass star with his quick shy smile. The star was fragile and sweet, its tiny ribbon encouraging donations to Toys for Tots. Emilia hung it in front of a bubble light so it could capture some sparkle and Des clapped his hands with pleasure.

Cordelia was sorting through the accumulated boxes of old ornaments searching for anything that looked child-made. Ben suspected that she thought they were made by his grandkids. He realized she didn't know these were the crafts of nieces and neighbors. Ben and Bea had never had children.

And so they had been safe from one danger – the Regans and Edmunds of the world. He looked around at folks from the building and streets all around, at friends from Arlington and Somerville and Melrose, and realized that he and his wife had never needed children. Their family was chosen, people who mattered to them, some younger, some older. The most recent neighbors stood beside friends who had been a part of that original plot to put Benedict and Beatrice together and others who had stood around the bed at her final curtain call. It was a party with a purpose, but was also a pretty wonderful party. And his Christmas tree would be trimmed.

The music up-ticked, just as Ariel suggested, and now tinsel was flung on the tree with sweet abandon and giggles. Amiens' sings in *As You Like It*:

> *Heigh-ho, sing heigh-ho! Unto the green holly,*
> *Most friendship is feigning, most loving mere folly.*

Not here and not tonight. The Shakespeare Reader read his gathering with warmer eyes. As for mistletoe? The baleful mistletoe of *Titus Andronicus* was anything but baleful in this company. Once noticed, there were maneuverings to come under its dangling or to stay clear with earnest or feigned fear. Horatia and Tony came in, and she slipped her ornament, a tiny pair of silver handcuffs, on a high branch of the Douglas fir. She smiled at Ben broadly.

Finally came the sharp knock awaiting no answer but drawing the attention of everyone. A flourish threw the door open, and with good-humored natural flamboyance Thello made his entrance, trays in hand and a cart stacked high with more trays jingling and juggling. So might the tinker's wagon arrive in another era to the applause of an entire village.

Delicious odors seduced the senses. A smell of roasted pork

– not just roast pork -- but pork roasted in a clay oven with herbs that mingled the Indian sub-continent and the so-called Indians of the North American one. It tempted even the birthright vegan to forswear. They were sewn on golden picks with mushrooms of exotic provenance and curls of purple onion. Nested beside them were tiny delectable ribs half-wrapped with a sprig of basil. Rabbit – it had to be rabbit -- and even Beatrix Potter would salivate as discreetly as possible.

There were cheeses – sweet cheeses to make a chocolate cake blush in shame, savory cheeses that tasted of camp fire and wind in the Rockies, melted cheeses on sesame flatbread that should be only available in the donors' lounges of the world's most famous opera houses. Cheeses.

Thello was no snob. Bowing to the trend-du-jour of bacon he'd wrapped not just scallops in it, but calamari so tender it was like chicken and ... yes, speaking of tastes-like-chicken there was his signature rattlesnake meat with the new skin of bacon and a mint leaf and a bright red cranberry bitter enough to wake the palate and proclaim in season's color the winding down of the year to the baby's navel of its holiness.

It was the food of magnificence, and it turned the entire crowd into a pack of beagles scenting a fox. A moment earlier, they had been acting in their own plays, as people do, whether they have gone to trim the tree of a Shakespeare Reader or not, and now they were united in an ensemble performance. A Zipcar named Desire.

Thello appeared not to notice the glazed eyes, the naked greed. He had eyes only for his host. "Ben, darling. What a beautiful tree – it is the grandest of trees! Cressida, sweetheart, aren't you just the best and furriest and most honest beggar in the room? They all envy you."

Cress played out her tricks in serial order. She sat and then played dead. She rolled over, put out her paw to shake and bowed her snout to her forefeet ... and then she started all over again. She loved Thello at all times for his gentle hands and the way he always smelled meaty-delicious. It was in his skin, in his hair – he had an aura to allure a carnivora. And Thello never forgot the dogs in his fandom – he had a bag in his pocket just for her. He lifted his expressive eyebrows to Ben and receiving a nod, gave her a large piece of meat, prepared just for her – nearly rare, scented of wood smoke and without any fancy sauces.

Amazingly enough, she returned his fine courtesy by taking it gently in her jaws and removing herself to a quiet corner to savor it. Having received this, her tithe, she didn't bother them again.

There was no need of passing trays. The guests came forward to pay homage to the food. There were different fashions in genuflection – some took a little plate, heaped it high and then retreated to a tray table as if to a cave, while others staked out a defensible position within arm's reach of the cart. Others, Horatia and Tony among them, were sampling each item singly but in community, an ad hoc gourmet club, commenting on savor and flavor while guessing the combinations of ingredients. Their attentiveness was somewhere between eucharist and foodie blog.

Thello was that rare thing – a chef who really doesn't care whether folks clear their palates between bites – drink Pellegrino water or just more creamy eggnog or cider. They could eat slowly or shovel it in. They could - horror – let it cool down while they talked of something else. He never judged those who ate his food. He had been hungry as a child and he never forgot. The kid inside him was just pleased when what he fed people pleased them. Tonight Thello grinned from ear to ear.

Ben waited for his young friend's greeting. Thello always prepared some improvisation on a Shakespeare line so that Ben understood the food was for him – it was endearing and rare behavior for a celebrity. Thello, like Horatia, had no upbringing that included the Bard. He cleared his throat, *"You love me for the dishes I have passed, and I love you that you did pity them."*

"*Othello!* Well done, though if you follow that story line along you may murder me for suspicion that I did hare after the rib of another man's rabbit."

"I would not murder you, and, you, Ben, would never chase another cook's appetizers."

"True, enough – that much a fool I am not!"

Another testimony to his humility, Thello always called himself "cook" rather than chef, as if he were still the young apprentice at a subway sushi bar and not the imaginative creator of the food of feasts, the employer of a small mob of sous-chef and line cooks and waitpersons and dishwashers and several slinky hostesses and hosts.

He was glowing with heat and satisfaction and dipped himself a cup of eggnog, giving praise where praise was due, for Ben's eggnog was holiday in a glass. He didn't need to serve the appetizers. He made many and all would disappear. The party picked up tempo with the infusion of blood and protein. Horatia wandered over and asked to be introduced. Ben raised his eyebrows in query and, imperceptibly, she shook her bright head. Ben introduced her by name as an old friend. If Thello spoke to Carol he would discover she was a homicide detective but for now she was anonymous, effusive and specific in her compliments – enough that he knew she knew something about food. They were smiling and chatting and Ben was thinking about moving to another cluster of guests, when Thello stopped him. He turned with pleasure to the big fir. He cleared his throat and spoke hesitantly.

"I brought you an ornament for your tree."

"Thello, you brought the party! You shouldn't have brought anything else!"

"Well I made it for you. It's simple." He handed over a little velvet bag, and Ben opened the tiny drawstring and dropped the contents onto his palm. It was a beautiful demitasse spoon and the handle was twisted once around and then shaped into a hanger. It was exquisite.

"I don't really have the right tools but I just used my hands to turn it and bend it. I do think I made it pretty smooth, almost circular." To the eye it was perfectly round and the twist made it glint in the light. Ben and Horatia looked at one another. It would take very strong fingers to bend silver so carefully. But this spoon wasn't silver – it was stainless steel.

"Thank you so much, I will treasure it – a spoon from the friend who always makes me kiss my spoon! Now go and play with children your own age."

Ben hung it himself. He heard a slight crunch and looked down at scattered fragments of glass. The little glass star was crushed, ground into the carpet. Ben bent over and saw a clear indentation. Boot heel. Ian had been standing here, swaying, pretending to admire the tree only a few moments earlier. He was wearing boots.

Ben felt cold.

Emily was at his elbow with his dustpan. How did women know where these things are in other people's houses? "Such a pity. I thought it was so secure. I don't think you need to tell the young man it's broken," she murmured. "Accidents happen."

He smiled at her with his party face and kept darker thoughts to himself.

Ben's guests were easing away regretfully from the empty cart. Thello planned to wait half an hour and then replace the meat and cheese – well, any that might remain -- with fruit and trim-the-tree balls of sherbet complete with silver-sugar hook. Ariel, barista to the core, was replenishing eggnog and cider and had even found a few bottles of wine for those who didn't think they had been to a party if they didn't drink wine.

Some danced; some hunted mistletoe.

Thello started across the room and then suddenly stopped, a cloud passing over his face, viselike hands opening and closing. Ben followed his gaze and saw Des, all laughs and sparkling eyes, leaning into a joke of one of the Demetrii. At the moment, Ben couldn't remember what this young man's real name was – but he categorized him as Demetrius rather than Lysander because he was the sort of boy who was always chasing after somebody else's true love.

Des was as short as Thello was tall, as fair as Thello was dark. He was no more than twenty-three, while Thello was in his mid thirties. Des was, even in a room of the young and bright and quick-witted, an ornament, a shining one.

He was shining into someone else's face as innocently as if he were playing a part. As Ben and Horatia watched, Ian Hunter sidled up to Thello and started speaking softly and confidentially. He had his phone out and was showing photos to the chef.

Ben turned to Horatia, "I fear he is saying something like, *'Des did deceive his former lover coming with you.'* To which Thello is responding, *'Villain, be sure thou prove my love a whore. Be sure of it; give me the ocular proof; or, by the worth of mine eternal soul thou hadst been better have been born a dog than answer my waked wrath.'"*

Horatia looked at him and her eyebrows rose. "Whatever. I think the conversation is going like this. Ian to Thello, 'You sure he's not hooking up with that guy from the third floor, one that's always hanging around? Gay bar pick up once is gay bar pick up always.' Thello's reply comes out, 'You say something like that, damn well better prove it ... But do you really think so?'"

"Exactly what I said."

She exaggerated her shrug.

With Thello's entrance all eyes had followed him. In any crowd, his celebrity entranced. When he was present, few noticed his roommates. Des didn't mind, since he was unconscious of his own beauty. Des and Thello were a lovely couple and Ben thought without interference they could stay together a long time. He was frustrated. "I can see it – the shape of the crime."

"If I responded to the shape of crimes in people's hearts, everyone would be incarcerated. Sorry. This time you need another authority figure." Horatia drifted over to Carol and her tall Titania with a happy greeting.

Another authority. O Beatrice, what masque can we stage? What guilts of the past can we exploit?"

And like a breath in his ear, the ear without the expensive hearing aid that let him listen to more of little matter than he had ever wished to hear, a breath of voice floated in. "Leave it to us, you never had a hand for subtle words or deceiving ways."

He turned startled, and only Ariel was there, a choice of drinks in her hands.

"Did you say something?"

"A woman's plot is always best, trust us to shape the villains test."

"What?"

"Nothing." Ariel shrugged. "Just something I heard on the wind. Relax, Ben. I have it on the best authority that you should not worry."

"But I do worry, I worry …"

But she was gone, having decidedly left the latte in his outstretched hand instead of the eggnog. She twirled in the center of the room, eggnog held high until the long brown arm of a Helena claimed it.

"… Ariel, Horatia I think …"

But there was no one there except there was still a voice in his ear, "*I wonder that you will still be talking, Signor Benedict: nobody marks you.*"

He froze and did not move a muscle. "Bea…"

But no. It must be Emilia, who was at his elbow showing him a tiny silver crèche that the clergywoman from the neighboring Methodist church had brought. He nodded approval and she went to hang it while he searched the crowd for Rev. Gemma. She stood by Thello's cart across the noisy room and caught his eye. He smiled his enthusiasm for the beautiful gift and mouthed "Thanks."

Quick as Rev. Gemma turned away, he heard the whisper come again, "*I took no more pains for those thanks than you take pains to thank me: if it had been painful, I would not have come.*"

Ben looked around surreptitiously. No one was nearby now at all. But he had heard the words clearly and they were Beatrice's

89

lines, *Much Ado* lines. Or not. After all, they were lines that anyone might say and probably were saying somewhere in this room. The hearing aid. It must be the hearing aid.

Ian. He must think about Ian and Thello and Des, not himself, himself in love, and certainly not himself crazy.

"You are no less than a stuffed man: but for the stuffing, well, we are all mortal."

"You're dead!" God the woman was irritating.

"They swore that you were well-nigh dead for me."

"I was. I am. You are. Why are you haunting me in the middle of a party?"

"You want me to go away? *I would have stayed here and called it a happy hour: I was about to protest I love you."*

Talking to no one, he was making a spectacle of himself. Ben started to fold into a chair where perhaps his internal dialogue would be less noticeable. Halfway down he felt hands under his armpits hoisting him up again.

"Do not you love me?"

"Beyond the script, my dear. Beyond anybody's script. It is you, isn't it, my darling, or is it just a replaying of empty lines by my heart so long lonely it's begun to twin itself with you?"

"No, not till a hot January."

"Bea, Beatrice, sweet jest-maker, these three years I've waited for you and you haven't come. Now you will have your jade's revenge when my friends and neighbors cart me away to a mental health unit."

"That won't happen if you just listen. I know, it's a struggle for you."

"But, will you come...?"

"First the masque – stand then with the women, like your namesake Benedict was willing to do when an innocent lover was maligned."

"I know the play." Irritated.

"Both plays, darling – they have the same plot."

"Certainly not! They are completely ... well, you're right. But they end very ..."

And suddenly Ben was surrounded by partygoers, and the sweetest breath that ever blew in one man's ear was still. And gone. Gone again and that was a December-bleak new loss, but yet, crazy or not, she'd been there. He gulped sobering latte, careless of future sleep and looked around, alert again.

Midwinter's night was stirring the fairies. Just as Ben thought he was set to intercept the ex-Marines, deep in the kind of conversation that excludes all others, and moves the plot along to violence when love is mixed with doubt, and betrayal is the greatest and the deepest fear. And what plot doesn't have it so? The line between *Othello* and *Much Ado* is thin - far thinner than those great herald-words "tragedy" and "comedy" would seem to announce.

Ben wanted to fix this as-yet-unrealized homicide, but could not see how to do it and neither, obviously, could the local constabulary. She found her way to his side again, her smile a sign that she was sated from the appetizers but with a curious expression on her face that made him fear that she might have witnessed his rather prolonged conversation with the air.

He gave a little chagrined shrug and lifted up his caffeinated beverage. "Time for the host to tip the tipsy back to vertical. I've been enjoying myself rather too much. It's almost the hour for me to watch who exits stage right with car keys. You, I hope are having a legitimately wicked time with your abstemious escort."

"By which you mean -- Tony doesn't drink."

"As I said."

"Or not. You are right, you know, about that light-haired stocky guy with the tats. He smells like trouble and maybe you have the inside on what kind of trouble, but I still don't think there is a damn thing I can do about it."

"I'm afraid you're right, but I am just glad you confirm my instincts."

"It's not like the Lear business. You nailed that."

"It was too late for him, Harry."

Harriet smiled. Everyone likes a nickname, but she also liked it when he remembered her real one.

Ben considered. Maybe this was no mystery for running through the streets, banging on a door, saving a poisoned young woman. He hadn't been too late for Cordelia. But for Des and Thello, he had a small hope it would be better served by illusions. Decorating a tree. Letting, for once, the much ado be about nothing. Summoning a powerful season where no real harm is done so hallowed and so gracious is the time. Well, spirits stir.

And maybe witches take.

Ian and Thello were still bent in deep conversation, but Thello's hands at his side were opening and closing in fists. Both men were damaged by the devastations they had witnessed, but one had found a way to feed people, to love people, and the other turned dark at heart. Ben would interrupt them. He gave Horatia a crooked smile and started across the room. Too slow. Titania swooped in from the shadows, regal, if slightly eggnog-impaired. From the corner of his eye he had the idea that Ariel had pushed her.

He was close enough to hear with his expensive and excellent device, better suited for guest eavesdropping than ghost channeling. He stopped and contemplated the scrabble board. The word was "Hero."

Esther Huso was as tall as Thello and as dark. "Good evening, gentlemen, so well met. My good Thello, we are truly graced by the delicacies of your table, but now you must let me sweep away your companion. You've done enough to energize the social joys of the night, and Des, who has been singing your praises all this evening long and moping for fear you'd never come to his side is just about wilted by the energetic chatter of small and fluttering Peaseblossoms and Cowslips fluttering around him not for himself, but because he is the reflection of your fame. Pity your sweet and faithful boy. Go to him before he languishes quite away."

No, she did not say Peaseblossom or Cowslip, but the rude

expressions she did use made it obvious she was all-so-lightly demeaning the young and flighty in the crowd.

Thello looked startled and eyed Ian who must have portrayed Des's evening in quite a different spirit. Titania cupped a hand rather securely under Iago's elbow "And you my dear, you are going to be my companion for a lovely talk about ... hmm Kabul. I understand you're quite the expert. An exotic place and a place of sadness." Her eyebrows curved like small perfect wings and Ian tried to slide away, suspecting she knew more about him than he wanted. Then, almost visibly, the thought registered that he must prevent this slightly tipsy African lady who knew something about him from talking to other guests, most especially Thello. As self-protection kicked in, he let her lead him away to a love seat in the corner.

Then there was a bit of magic. Just a very little bit. Titania looked up to see mistletoe hanging over that very well-named love seat and shuddered. It vanished in an instant. Ben started, but Horatia, again at his side, pointed at Prof O in her line of vision on the opposite side of the room. He had snapped his fingers. The sprig of mistletoe was in them. Titania mouthed "Thank you" silently toward the old magician who, in spite of his cloudy thoughts of revenge, did not miss much. She sat down regally to draw her dark net around Iago.

The wild card, witch, woman. The Deus ex machina.

Thello steered a course across the room past well-wishers who wanted to smell the aroma of his fame. He smiled but slipped undeterred away and when he reached Des, the younger man's smile lit up the room. Even the Christmas tree itself faded. Thello reached down and gently kissed his lover's upturned forehead and, for a moment, the room was theirs alone.

And on the night went, around the Douglas fir, but now with pairings as sweet and in most cases as insubstantial as the mandatory Act Five of a comedy. The blowing of winter winds did not echo human unkindness. Tony and Horatia danced and neither of them needed an alcoholic drink for the courage. Thello and Des danced and it was on YouTube before the clock struck twelve.

Calvin dropped by, crashing the emotional barometer, of course, and ending Emilia's enterprise of drawing out the professor's charm. Prospero was back in character the minute Cal appeared. To Ben's enormous relief, before she could turn her sights back to him, Emilia decided it was her bedtime and that she must be off. Ben managed to give her a nice parcel of Mrs. Garrity's cookies and a couple pieces of exquisite fruitcake that no one else would touch. Emilia cast a last regretful look at Prospero, sunk down into a chair to brew again his low pressure-but-never-extinguished weather.

Ben air-kissed his book-club buddy and whispered, "Be persistent." He wasn't sure she heard it, but she smiled and left.

Cal, oblivious to his casting as a villain, was neighborly and glowing from some academic honor or new publication that he needed to fame-drop in a dozen ears. He stayed barely a half hour and left as well.

"Can't you do anything about that?" Ariel asked. "Great-uncle is a train wreck waiting to happen."

"A shipwreck rather, and maybe he must go through it, Ariel, my dear. He's started up a case in court, I understand."

"He should get free of it all."

"And do what? Sit in the apartment pretending that he is writing a book? Play with magic and maybe light the damn building on fire around all of us?"

"You know about that?"

"I can guess well enough of his experiments from what I see and hear."

"Therapy would be cheaper, easier on the china, the counters. He almost blew up the toilet, you know."

She looked so serious and he paused long enough that in a moment they were both laughing and she went to serve someone else a drink and didn't noticed that their conversation was never finished.

Maybe he could do something. Or maybe he was just a nosy old man with a hobby of interfering that he dressed up in period costume.

Thello served the fruit and sherbet balls. They melted into the company with pleasure. Ben had put lights on a timer to dim down now and they were making the crowd sleepy. Slowly they began to leave – his lovely guests, his friends.

Ian Hunter left first with a determined look on his face. He bid Ben farewell – he had the offer of a very interesting job and he was flying out of the country tomorrow. Mercenary? Trainer of troops? Ben wondered, and thought about the power and reach of Titania the ruthless queen. She may not have been rescuing Thello and Des so much as scenting a mortal who could do some devious bidding. There were villains in many Shakespeare plays and Ben hoped his party had not transposed an evil from one into another.

Get free of it all! Ariel's advice to her uncle should work for Ben. The guy had a job offer. Better than being a waiter in a war buddy's fancy restaurant. If his only skill was being a soldier, there were employers for that. And maybe the job was something completely different.

Cordelia. Carol, his dear, perhaps an Emilia in waiting, but kind and sweet, shook her head ever so slightly as she and Titania swept out. She leaned over, *"And yet not so; since I am sure my love's more richer than my tongue."*

"Not going to work for you?"

"Not this much drama, but it was a grand night."

He kissed her. "You deserve the very best of loves and you will find it. But perhaps the grand night is not over. Take this fairy queen full of the wicked eggnog home ... a taste of the greenwood even if you don't want to live in the forest."

"Old man, what do you know of such things?" but she smiled slyly.

"What does her kanga say?"

"The jina says, 'I won't revenge but I won't forget.' Why couldn't it be something like '*Mkipendana mambo huwa sawa* — Everything is all right if you love each other.'" Carol laughed. She'd be all right.

The younger party guests left. Some had the partners they wanted and some wanted the ones they did not have, and that was as it was always going to be. Horatia or Harry or Dogsy and her dear Tony felt the lure of the babysitter, and Horatia kissed him as well. Ben wondered if being a Shakespeare Reader meant some nights all the heroines kissed you before their exits?

He bowed and spoke to Tony, *"For since my dear soul was mistress of her choice and could of men distinguish, her election hath sealed thee for herself."*

Horatia replied, surprising him as well, *"Well, my lord: if anyone steal aught the whilst this play is playing, and 'scape detecting, I will pay the theft."*

"Meaning," said Tony, "Harry's a hell of a detective and I'm her guy?"

Ben took a deep breath, "Exactly. I think with absolutely no credit to ourselves, this play has righted itself, the spheres are in good order with the world, and we've been audience this time."

"And I've had a great evening. This is my favorite part of police work. The crime didn't happen, and we've done better than doughnuts."

"It is a gentle season, a time when such easy resolutions are in the air."

"You think he's off to trouble someone else?"

"Probably, and I, being relieved for my neighbor, sent him into the world."

"Honey, no crime, no time. Don't be so moody. It looked like he was leaving on his own two number tens. Be glad for what you have and what you have escaped. I am, most days! That's what makes a cop," she pointed at the tree's highest branch, "not handcuffs"

"Where shall we three meet again in thunder, lightning, or in rain? When the hurly-burly 's done, when the battle 's lost and won."

Now Tony was completely out of his depth. As a high school

teacher, he had a lot of experience with the feeling. However, the innuendos and quotations had gone on long enough. He was also the football coach and so gave that most universal of gestures, Time Out.

Ben laughed. "That's Macbeth."

Harry offered, "Well, if my 'reading' of the Boston sky is anything to go by – we shall meet in blizzard, ice, and frost, when the Advent wreath is done, when Aggie's battle for her stocking's lost and won!"

Prospero sighed and unfolded from his chair in echo and gave Ben a long look under his craggy brows. He might in reality be as insightful as a post, but with those eyebrows he had a grand appearance of intelligence and mystery. He gave Ben's hand a particularly vigorous shake and left. Ariel had waggled her fingers at her great uncle in a gesture of "go to bed I'll be up in a moment."

Ben's heart was pierced suddenly and surprisingly to see it. With just such a sweet dismissal had Bea often sent him away. Love that was love never stopped hurting – sharp and precious. Every little light flounce of these young women reminded him how much he'd lost and ... just how much his joints were creaking right about now.

Peace, I will stop your mouth. What did he hear? Words he'd said to a woman now so insubstantial he only heard her in the echo of an Advent crowd. Or now. If you are here, Bea, really here, say something now.

"Sit, down. Relax. It was a lovely party. You should be pleased." Ariel meant it differently than Horatia had. She had no underlying agendas – sprites don't. Unless. But he wasn't going to think of that. What she knew was that Ben had wanted to throw a party in this busiest of all seasons at a moment's notice, and everyone had dropped their plans to come. She could tell him that and he would ascribe it to Thello's notoriety and cuisine, but, delicious as that was, they would have come without it. They would have come for Ben.

Ben sat down. The Douglas fir was lovely and to have new ornaments and new memories was a very good thing, a thing to be pleased with. It glowed lightly, and Ben genuinely hoped that Prospero had kept his experiments off the tree.

Ariel went for minimalist. "Everyone had a wonderful time." She looked at the Shakespeare Reader. She had a quotation for him. He would like it. *"We are such stuff as dreams are made on, and our little life is rounded with a sleep."* He looked up and smiled at her.

Ariel smiled in return. Took the last glass of eggnog out of his drooping hand and set it down safely on the small lamp table. She found an afghan and rested it on his knees. And then either Ariel left and Bea recited or Ariel was still there and trying on some Hamlet – it is, after all, everyone's Shakespeare play.

> *Some say that ever 'gainst that season comes*
> *Wherein our Savior's birth is celebrated,*
> *This bird of dawning singeth all night long;*
> *And then, they say, no spirit dare stir abroad,*
> *The nights are wholesome, then no planets strike.*
> *No fairy takes, nor witch hath power to charm,*
> *So hallowed and so gracious is the time.*

But the Shakespeare Reader was dozing in his chair.

ABOUT THE AUTHOR

Maren C Tirabassi is the author of eighteen books, many published by The Pilgrim Press, including the recent **From the Psalms to the Cloud – Connecting to the Digital Age** with Maria Mankin. She is a former Poet Laureate of Portsmouth, New Hampshire. She can be found at the poetry and global worship blog **Gifts in Open Hands** at www.giftsinopenhands.wordpress.com.

Maren has been a United Church of Christ pastor in Massachusetts and New Hampshire since 1980. She facilitates creative writing workshops in a range of settings from recovery group to senior center, correctional facility to English Language Learning class. She lives with Don Tirabassi and Willie the beagle in Portsmouth. She is very fond of Christmas!

Made in the USA
Charleston, SC
22 October 2014